D0822770

ENEMY OF THE REALM

ENEMY OF THE REALM

A DRAGONS VS. DRONES NOVEL

WESLEY KING

RAZORBILL

An Imprint of Penguin Random House

RAZORBILL

An Imprint of Penguin Random House
Penguin.com

Copyright © 2017 Penguin Random House LLC

Penguin Random House supports copyright. Copyright fuels creativity, encourages diverse voices, promotes free speech, and creates a vibrant culture. Thank you for buying an authorized edition of this book and for complying with copyright laws by not reproducing, scanning, or distributing any part of it in any form without permission. You are supporting writers and allowing Penguin Random House to continue to publish books for every reader.

ISBN: 978-1-59514-799-8

Printed in the United States of America

1 3 5 7 9 10 8 6 4 2

Book design by Corina Lupp

This is a work of fiction. Names, characters, places, and incidents either are the product of the author's imagination or are used fictitiously, and any resemblance to actual persons, living or dead, businesses, companies, events, or locales is entirely coincidental.

For Mom and Dad,
who gave me everything I required to
set off in search of magic.

Good news: I found it.

Prologue

They appeared on the horizon like a giant, monstrous arrow unleashed from the ground. With his keen eyes, sharper than any eagle's, Lourdvang counted five: four Trackers on the flanks, angular and raven black, and a much larger Destroyer at the lead—white as snow and bristling with weaponry. He had seen the same formation many times before. They had come to kill.

"Nathaniel!" he growled. "Time to leave."

Nathaniel looked back, a bundle of supplies slung over his shoulders. He was only fourteen, but he looked much older—corded with muscle and cold blue eyes that had seen too much devastation at such a young age. They flashed with anger now. "Drones?"

Lourdvang blew a puff of black smoke from his nostrils. "Yes. And in a death formation. I don't think they're here for us—they have come to destroy Rennia. But we have to get back home . . . now."

The Resistance fighters and their families had taken refuge in Forost, the ancestral home of the Nightwings, but their encampment was desperately short on food. Lourdvang and Nathaniel had volunteered to do the supply runs after the last pair was gunned down by drones. This was only their second time venturing out, and both knew the terrible danger.

Nathaniel cursed and turned back to the shop owner. "Get to shelter," he warned, before heading out onto the street to alert the people of Rennia. He waved his arms and yelled as loud as he could. "Everyone, find shelter!"

They didn't need to be told twice. So many villages in the outskirts of Dracone had already been destroyed, and they all knew that Rennia would eventually meet the same fate. They had delayed, reluctant to leave. But the storm was finally coming.

Screams filled the street as mothers grabbed their children, and everyone hurried away from the city center, flooding into basements or squat, brick shops for cover. Lourdvang knew bricks and basements would not protect them from the terrible firepower of the drones. The smartest people headed away from the village entirely, running for the sprawling meadows. If they were fast enough, they might escape.

Lourdvang lowered himself to the ground so that Nathaniel could reach him. "Get on!"

The desire to protect the villagers burned hot in Lourdvang, but he knew this was a fight he could not win. He felt like a defenseless rabbit. It was time to run back to their hole.

Nathaniel donned his black fire-protective gloves—along with the full suit he already wore—and raced up Lourdvang's back with the precious supplies. He sat down at the base of Lourdvang's long neck and grabbed onto a protruding scale, digging his fingers in for a better grip. Even with Nathaniel's heavy gloves, Lourdvang knew it would be searing hot that far beneath his scales. But Nathaniel held on tightly, never making a sound.

Lourdvang was just about to take off when the first missile struck the village. It slammed into a large home, erupting in a plume of fire and ash and sending splintering wood everywhere. The ground shook with the impact, and Lourdvang could see villagers crash into the dirt, covering their heads and crying out for help. But help wasn't coming. Even Lourdvang, a fully grown Nightwing, was completely outmatched.

He spread his great wings and leapt into the air just as the next missile struck. He flapped with all of his strength, trying to escape the barrage as more screams echoed in the distance. He looked back as a fresh wave of projectiles tore the village to shreds. Structures were collapsing, homes were vanishing, people were dying.

Lourdvang flew toward the clouds. Thankfully he and Nathaniel were not the targets today. But that day would come soon.

Lourdvang and Nathaniel watched silently as drones completed their methodical work, destroying yet another beautiful Draconian village. Flames seemed to consume everything. Lourdvang turned away and looked toward his destination, letting the cold moisture of the clouds wash over him as if to try to clean the memory away, though he knew it wouldn't work. It never did.

As he sailed above the cloud cover under the brilliant morning sun, one thought continued to haunt Lourdvang:

Where were Marcus and Dree?

Chapter 1

The raging wind subsided into a whisper, and Marcus, Dree, and George were left standing alone in the middle of the carnage. Coffee cups and newspapers littered the street around them, twisting in the last bit of breeze, while the hordes of frazzled commuters standing around them were trying to fix their windblown hair and figure out what had just happened. Marcus hadn't realized the portal was going to deliver them back to Arlington right in the thick of the busy morning rush hour. They had just appeared out of nowhere in front of hundreds of people.

"What . . . where . . ." Dree said, clearly too stunned to think.

A few commuters were staring at them now, and Marcus

saw them reaching for their cell phones. Police attention or, even worse, a photo uploaded to the Internet were the last things that they needed right now. Francis could be watching, and George was wanted as an American traitor.

"Let's move," Marcus said, grabbing an astounded Dree's arm.

Marcus pulled Dree around the busy street corner onto Fifth, his father trailing close behind them. Marcus was still soaked from the storm during their frantic escape from Dracone, and his clothes were clinging uncomfortably to his skin. He could feel water sloshing around in his shoes. He blinked as water snaked its way around his gray eyes.

Marcus slowed down a little, trying to get his bearings in the busy rush hour crowds; and Dree came to a full stop, looking around the street wide-eyed and disbelieving. Marcus couldn't really blame her. Arlington, Virginia, was about as different from her home in Dracone as possible: Cars whizzed past, honking as they made their way through commuter traffic, while men and women in business attire walked by, cell phones held up to their ears. The air was full of riotous noise: horns and conversations and the low, steady thunder of thousands of footsteps on the concrete.

"It's so . . . busy," Dree murmured, staring up at a towering glass skyscraper.

Marcus glanced back at her. She was reacting just like he had when he first appeared in Dracone a month earlier, staring out in wonder at the strange, industrializing medieval world. It had been a whirlwind ever since.

Despite their escape from Francis and his drones after the attack on the palace, Marcus knew Dracone was still in grave danger. Francis not only had his factory of drones churning out more and more of the deadly weapons, but he now had Baby Hybrid. She had been damaged in the attack, but not irreparably, and Francis could easily get her back in the air. Marcus's stomach twisted whenever he thought of his and Dree's prize creation in the hands of that madman. With the hybrid on his side and a fleet of drones, Francis would be almost unstoppable in Dracone. Only the Egg could save them now. With its power to generate supposedly limitless energy, they would be able to build an even more powerful hybrid.

"Uh-oh," George said.

Marcus followed his eyes and saw a policewoman pushing her way through the crowds holding a walkie-talkie to her mouth and with her second hand on her billy club. She was heading right for them. Marcus weighed his options. If they were arrested, George would be recognized for sure.

"Follow me," Marcus said.

He turned and led the three of them right into the crowd. He pushed and jostled his way through, eliciting some angry mutters and dark stares, and spared a look back. The policewoman was still visible—though just the top of her cap.

"Stay low," Dree warned, noticing the same thing.

They hurried ahead, George clearly laboring, and Marcus finally spotted their chance: a narrow alley tucked between two older buildings. He pushed through another knot of people, slouching just enough to keep his head below theirs, and then veered left into the alley. He rounded a dumpster and crouched behind it, where he was joined a second later by Dree and George. George was breathing heavily, and he grabbed at his sides as they waited. Marcus knew that if the policewoman came down the alley, they would be spotted in seconds. And now they looked *very* guilty.

The seconds ticked by. Finally, Marcus risked a glance. The policewoman was gone.

"I think we're all right," he said.

"Why are they chasing us?" Dree asked.

"She probably came to investigate the storm and someone gave her our description," George replied. "Which should be easy," he said wryly, gesturing at Dree's Draconian clothes.

Marcus had to agree. She was wearing a worn leather jerkin over a forest-green tunic, a looping brown belt, and beige pants singed with fire. They had decided it was her most "Earthlike" outfit, but it was still a stretch for downtown Arlington.

"We'll just try to stay out of sight," Dree muttered.

Marcus checked the skies warily as they hurried down the alley, trying to put some distance between them and the commuters who had first seen them appear. He worried that drones could be watching them too. It was likely that Francis still had some on this side of the portal.

They had to get off the streets. They turned out of the alley and kept moving.

Marcus saw that Dree was slowing down again, and he pulled her along. His father was still struggling to keep up as well, already winded and clutching at his sides. It had been eight years since George had been on Earth, and he had spent the last three or four of those trapped in a secret Draconian dungeon, strapped to a chair. During that time, he had withered away to the pale, emaciated man who was now jogging to keep up. He was like a ghost of the father Marcus remembered as a child.

Marcus led them down another side street, and the crowd thinned out a little.

"You all right?" Marcus asked his father, concerned.

"Fine," he wheezed. "Just haven't exercised in a while, I guess."

"How far is this safe house with the Egg?" Dree asked.

"A few miles," George said, scooping up a crumpled newspaper strewn on the ground. His eyes locked on the date as if it was some sort of illusion. "But we need to be smart about this. And I'll need Jack's help to get it."

Marcus frowned. "You never mentioned that before. Do we really have to get Uncle Jack involved? We'll be putting him in danger."

"He knows the risks," George said. "In fact, he knows a lot more than you think." A horn blared out on the street, and Marcus jumped. He scanned the skies again.

"Keep moving," he said curtly. As they started hurrying down the street again, he glanced at his father. "You really think this can be done?"

"We have no choice but to find out. We're stealing from the CIA, Marcus. It's not going to be easy. We're talking about armed guards, cameras, security doors. The place is a fortress."

"Great," Marcus muttered, feeling the morning sun beating down on his head.

Dree gestured at a woman who pushed past them, her eyes locked on her cell phone.

"You mentioned the Internet before. Is that what all these people are doing?"

"Pretty much," Marcus said. He turned back to his father. "Well, we still have to move fast. Who knows what's happening to the Draconian people as we speak."

George lowered his voice. "I know, but we won't do them any good in jail. Once we get the Egg, we'll go back right away. Then we have to worry about getting your Baby Hybrid back, or at least building a new one. The Egg will make it a lot easier—you won't need to worry about a power source. I believe the Egg might also make Lourdvang and the other dragons stronger."

"There are an awful lot of *ifs* in our plan," Marcus said.

"We'll have to make do," Dree replied.

"Agreed," George said. "We have to get to Jack's house first."

"All right," Marcus said. "If you're sure that's the only

way. Let's get a cab. It's a few blocks away."

Marcus tried to wave down a cab, but it just kept driving.

Dree watched in fascination as the car sped by. "Those are wonderful. How do they work?"

"It's . . . complicated," Marcus muttered, too focused on getting a ride to pay Dree much attention.

Dree tilted her head and studied the passing cars. "I'm guessing a combustible fuel moves the pistons, generating torque for the wheels."

Marcus turned to her, stunned. "How did you—"

"It's a bit like dragon fire, really," Dree said. "I'd love to take one apart if we ever get the time. Maybe I could even build one."

"Once we win the war, we can tear apart all the cars you like," Marcus said.

He stepped to the side of the road and started waving at the next cab, letting his father scan through the newspaper. Marcus looked around the busy streets, remembering that this city had once been his home. Now it seemed almost alien to him. The crisp black suits, the din of horns and ringing cell phones and rumbling city buses—it was so chaotic and frenzied, and yet it also seemed so . . . lifeless. Ordinary. Marcus realized that he yearned for Dracone. He even missed Dracone's air: fresh and alive and brimming with energy.

Just as a cab pulled up, something flashed across Marcus's vision. It moved quickly between the buildings, soaring like a large pigeon.

But it had been circular, and the black hull had glinted noticeably in the morning sun. *A Surveyor drone.* Marcus turned to the others. "It's time to go."

Sun reflected off the cab windows as Marcus, Dree, and George rolled through the city. Marcus sat in the front, his eyes locked on the skyline. He hadn't seen any other drones, and he hoped the drone sighting had just been in his imagination. But he also knew Francis wanted that Egg desperately and wouldn't hesitate to track Marcus and the rest on Earth.

Marcus didn't tell the others what he had seen. He didn't want to alarm them when they had other things to worry about. George, sitting in the back of the cab, continued to read his newspaper. He occasionally snorted or grunted in disbelief, but mostly he used the paper to keep his face hidden from the driver. It may have been eight years, but George was still infamous.

Dree's wide-eyed face, on the other hand, was in full view as she gaped at every new thing they passed: strip malls with their garish neon signs, bustling coffee shops, and skyscrapers glinting in the morning sun. She stared in wonder at a man eating a burger in his car next to them— making the man look very uneasy—and then gasped aloud when she saw a plane fly over the city.

"Marcus—"

"Just a passenger plane," Marcus said quickly, "flying people around. No big deal."

She settled back into her seat and went back to staring out the window.

"So simple," she said, watching as a cyclist pedaled by. "I can't wait to build one of those."

"Priorities," Marcus reminded her, giving the driver a forced smile.

But clearly the driver had seen plenty of strange things in his cab, because he barely seemed to notice. They were nearly out of the downtown core now and would be arriving at Marcus's old apartment in minutes. Marcus thought about Uncle Jack. Would he be furious with Marcus for taking off so suddenly? For all Marcus knew his face was printed on milk cartons around the city as a missing child, and his uncle had been out looking for him ever since.

What would Jack say when they arrived?

"Jack is going to be surprised when he sees you," he murmured, glancing at his father.

George's eyes flicked up to Marcus over the paper. "I don't doubt it."

"What are you going to tell him?"

"The truth."

Marcus turned to him, surprised. "You are?"

"Like I've been trying to tell you, Jack knows more than you think. In fact, I doubt he even told anyone you were . . . on vacation."

"Really?"

George nodded. "Trust me, he knows where you went. And he will be more than willing to help us."

13

Marcus frowned. "So he . . . knew everything?"

George clearly heard the tone in his voice, and his eyes darted to the driver. "A lot."

Marcus felt a little heat prickling under his skin. Jack had lied to him his entire life.

"He only did as I instructed," George said calmly. "And what he thought was best."

"He didn't trust me to know anything, you mean," Marcus muttered.

"It was a little more complicated than that, Marcus."

Marcus knew it wasn't the time for this talk. But he was hurt by the revelation. All those times he had asked about his father. And where his dad had gone. Jack had known the truth.

"I deserved to know," he said.

"And now you do," George said. "You were just a boy."

"You don't know what I was like," Marcus said, a bit more sharply than he intended.

George sighed. "No, I guess I didn't. And I'm sorry about that."

Marcus felt a little pang of guilt. "Well . . . I'm glad Jack won't be mad."

George lifted the paper again, though not before Marcus caught the hurt in his eyes.

"I'm sure he'll be relieved. He was your father more than I was."

Dree shifted in the back, obviously uncomfortable. "What's he like?"

"You're going to like him," Marcus said, as they stopped at a light. "He's . . . interesting."

"I like interesting people," she said wryly, staring at a fire hydrant. "Great idea. Obviously for water. Does that mean you have water systems running beneath the entire city? Fascinating. They must be very high pressure for that system to work. I wonder if I could create something like that for . . . home. Do you think I could take one apart—"

"Later," Marcus said, rubbing an exasperated hand through his hair.

As they turned onto Marcus's street, he started growing more and more excited to see the apartment. Even if it seemed like Marcus might belong in Dracone, he had still grown up in Arlington. He still missed his room and his friends and Jack. Marcus could just picture the look on his uncle's face when he told him he had ridden on a dragon.

He thankfully still had his wallet in his backpack and quickly paid the cab driver before leading them inside the building, nearly running with anticipation.

But Marcus's excitement faded the second he opened the apartment door. The place was in shambles: furniture had been upended and strewn around the room, drawers had been ransacked, and clothes were scattered everywhere. Marcus exchanged a concerned look with his father.

Uncle Jack was gone.

Chapter 2

Dree held up a shattered picture of Marcus, the only one she had found. He was much younger in the picture, with a goofy lopsided grin and big ears. It had been cast carelessly onto the ground, and she could feel the shards of glass under her boots. It seemed a bit silly considering the state of the apartment, but she couldn't keep herself from carefully placing it back on the table. She had already seen her house decimated by drones. Now Marcus's home had been ransacked too.

She could hear him frantically tearing through his bedroom now, while George searched Jack's room looking for any clues as to his whereabouts. Dree had taken the kitchen and living room, but she knew they were all probably searching in vain. Either Jack had cleared this place out, or someone else had. And they had done a very thorough job.

She wondered if Francis had any operatives in this world. She felt a flash of anger at the thought of him and his mocking, evil smile. Sometimes it was still hard to believe the popular prime minister was behind so much bloodshed and destruction. That he had broken Dree's father and was responsible for the murder of so many innocent dragons. And now he had Baby Hybrid. She felt heat pressing against her skin from inside and tried to calm down. It wouldn't be good to set anything on fire here. That wouldn't help Marcus's mood.

She glanced at the picture again, thinking about her own family. Were they okay? When she had left they were still living in a hidden cave, at her insistence, apart from her cowardly brother, Rochin. He was probably living down-town again, away from the slums that Francis was even now eradicating from the city limits. But she was desperately worried for Abi and her little brothers, and she knew Francis would love to get his hands on her family for leverage . . . or revenge.

And then there was Lourdvang.

She knew her other "little brother" would never stand to hide from the drones for long. He was a fighter, a protector—and that meant he was in danger. Dree didn't know what she would do if she ever lost him—the bond they shared as dragon and Rider meant everything to her. She had helped raise him from almost a newborn, back when he was the size of a dog. He had since grown into a powerful dragon, and she was proud of the leader he was becoming.

There was no time to dwell now, though, and Dree quickly resumed her search for clues. The faster they found the Egg, the faster they could get back to Dracone—to Lourdvang and Abi and everyone else—and rejoin the war.

She walked into the kitchen, scanning over the ransacked drawers littering the floor. Dree picked up a plate, wondering what it would have been like to live in a place like this, where everything was so advanced and clean and sterile. But she didn't feel the same magic here as in Dracone, the same visceral energy in the air and the wind. She wondered if it had been here once, and they had forgotten it in favor of these technological marvels—just like Francis was trying to do there. Whatever it was, Earth just felt cold and empty.

Suddenly, Dree heard footsteps coming from the hallway outside the apartment door. She froze, slowly placing the plate down and crouching beside the counter, out of view. She kept her eyes on the front door as it eased open and a portly blond boy stepped in, clearly trying to be stealthy. He wasn't really succeeding. His face was twisted in concentration as he gingerly tiptoed toward Marcus's bedroom. He took a peek inside, grinned, and prepared to charge through the door.

He never made it.

Dree exploded from behind the counter and tackled him, sending both of them sprawling across the room with a violent thud. Dree landed on top and pinned down his arms, her wiry arms flexing.

"Who are you?" she demanded.

"Ow," the boy moaned, grimacing and looking up at her. His cheeks immediately flushed red, and a few spotted scarlet hives appeared on his neck like chicken pox. "Am I dreaming?" he whispered.

Marcus rushed out from inside his bedroom. "Dree, what happ— *Brian*?"

"Hey, buddy," Brian said, still pinned to the floor.

For the first time since they landed on Earth, Marcus laughed. "It's okay, Dree. He's a friend of mine."

Dree quickly let Brian go, watching as the boy rubbed his rib cage. "Sorry about that," she said.

"She hits like a linebacker," Brian muttered.

"You have no idea," Marcus said, pulling his friend up off the ground. "It's good to see you."

"Yeah, thanks for leaving without any warning," Brian said. He glanced at Dree, flushed anew, and then lowered his voice and leaned in closer to Marcus. "Who's the babe?"

"I can hear you," Dree said.

George emerged from Jack's bedroom, tucking something into his pocket. "You must be Brian."

"*Mr. Brimley?*" Brian asked in amazement, looking between George and Marcus. "But . . . how . . . I mean . . . where . . . *you're alive?*"

"So far," George responded wryly.

"How did you know we were here?" Marcus asked Brian.

"Right." Brian plopped onto the couch, looking around. "This place is a mess. Was Jack a messy dude?"

"Brian, focus!" Marcus said.

"Sorry. Jack came over to my house two weeks ago. Showed up all inconspicuous, like a spy or something."

"He *is* a spy," George said.

"Oh," Brian said, frowning. "O . . . kay? Anyway, he told me that he was leaving, but if I saw you I should tell you that he went on a fishing trip. And I was like, *no offense, Jack, but shouldn't you be looking for Marcus instead of going fishing?* But he said you were fine. So I'm like, *where is he?* And he said you were visiting some family. And I go, *okay, cool, but it would have been nice to know.* And you know, dude, it *would* have been nice to know."

Dree smiled. She couldn't help but like Brian. He seemed permanently exasperated.

"So he went on a fishing trip?" Marcus asked, rubbing his forehead.

"Weird, right?" Brian said. "I mean, he doesn't really look like a fisherman. Oh, and before he left he gave me this little camera to set up outside in the hallway. It takes pictures when people walk by and sends it to my phone, and I caught a quick glimpse of you and ran over. Though I totally missed the girl you were with, which is surprising because . . ." He stopped. "Well, you know. Anyway, that's all I know. So how was the family visit? Was it to go see your dad in Russia? And are you going to explain who this girl is at some point or what?"

"I'm Dree," she said, extending a hand.

Brian broke out in hives as he shook her hand. "Brian," he murmured. "You have a strong grip."

George was now standing at the window, looking out at the parking lot thoughtfully. Marcus walked over to him. "Does Uncle Jack even fish?" Marcus asked.

"He's not on a fishing trip," George said. "It's a code we used before I left. It means that he's in trouble." George turned to Marcus, frowning.

"And it also means Brian isn't the only one who's been watching this apartment."

Chapter 3

George's grim words hung in the air for a moment, and then Brian looked at Marcus. "What does that mean? What trouble? Are the Russians here?"

Marcus followed his father's gaze out the window, scanning over the skyline. He was looking for a glint of white metal or a black shape on the horizon. Were the drones out there right now? Was Francis watching them? Or was it the CIA?

"What do we do now?" Marcus asked, ignoring Brian.

George sighed. "We go ahead as planned. The Egg is the priority. But without Jack's help, we'll need to gather more information. And that starts with scouting the location.

I was kind of relying on him to catch me up to speed on any changes."

Brian rubbed his forehead. "An *egg*? How is an egg more important than the fact that your uncle Jack is missing?"

"This isn't a normal egg," Dree said. "It's an ancient dragon relic full of indescribable power."

Brian stared at her for a moment, and then he turned to Marcus. "She's joking, right? Is she joking? Or . . . ?"

Marcus realized that he couldn't keep Brian in the dark any longer. "You'd better get comfortable," he said. "It's kind of a long story."

As Dree listened in and George did some research on Marcus's computer, Marcus sat down beside Brian and covered everything from the beginning: the drones, the portal, the group's journey to Dracone. It was almost hard for Marcus to believe it all himself, but Brian never interrupted.

After Marcus finished talking, Brian stared at him in silence for a bit. Then, a hint of recognition filled his eyes. "Is this why you kept melting Xboxes?" he asked. "Because you're not . . . you know, *from here*?"

"That only happened once," Marcus said, rolling his eyes. "And *that's* what you've taken away from everything I told you?"

Brian turned toward Dree. "So you're a Dragon Rider too?" he asked.

She nodded.

"This is the greatest thing ever!" Brian said excitedly. "So now you have to find the Egg to turn the tables against the evil dude Francis to save Dracone? And the Egg is full of *dragon* magic? I want in! How can I help?"

Dree giggled and Marcus just shook his head. "For now, you can just keep a secret."

"I can do that." Brian grinned. "Dragons? So cool. Except for the whole drone part." He paled and looked at the window. "Are they out there?"

"They won't risk exposing themselves until they have to," George said. "They'll wait until we make our move, and then they'll go in for the kill. When that happens, we'll just have to be ready to escape in a hurry."

"But first, the Egg," Marcus said, looking to his father for next steps.

"Exactly," George replied. "But we have to steal it from one of the most heavily guarded compounds in Arlington. Without Jack as our guide. All while being hunted by drones and the CIA. So settle in, we have a lot of planning to do."

George paused.

"Brian, this isn't your mission, and I won't put you in danger. You'll have to go home."

Brian looked like he wanted to argue, but the seriousness of the situation finally seemed to hit him. "Okay, but if you need anything—"

"We'll see you later, Brian," George said.

Brian saluted and hurried off, giving Dree one last flushed grin. The door shut behind him, and Marcus turned to Dree, shaking his head. "Sorry about that. He's a bit . . . weird around girls."

"And you're a regular charmer," she said sarcastically. "I like him." She turned to George, folding her arms. "So, what do we have to do?"

Once the sun set, Marcus, Dree, and George ventured out once again. They moved quickly through the streets, trying to stay clear of any lights, not that it really mattered for the drones. If Trackers were up there, Marcus knew there was infrared locked on him even now. But the group had done their best to stay out of view, and they had no choice but to keep moving. George needed to get a look at the CIA annex to see if the security perimeter had changed. If there were any new obstacles, they would have to alter their plans.

George made his way down another side alley, with Marcus and Dree trailing close behind.

"So how do you like Earth?" Marcus asked, glancing back at Dree.

Dree snorted. "It seems like a lot of hiding so far. But I do love the Internet."

She spent an hour that afternoon on the Internet, poring over all the information it had to offer. She quizzed Marcus on subjects spanning from global wars to celebrities to space exploration. She was amazed that athletes and movies stars were so popular, instead of soldiers and famous warriors. When she wasn't surfing the Web she was busy inspecting every piece of technology she could get her hands on—including disassembling the television. She was also clearly getting very anxious to get back to Dracone.

"We'll get the Egg soon," Marcus said, guessing at her thoughts. "We have to be careful."

"Every minute is another one that Francis could be finding my family," she pointed out. Ahead of them, George was looking around constantly, getting his bearings. They were moving through an empty parking lot lit only faintly by a few dim streetlights.

"I know," Marcus said. "We'll get back there soon, don't worry."

"What was it like to live here?" Dree asked, staring up at a building twinkling with a hundred office lights.

Marcus thought for a moment. "I don't know. Fine. Sometimes I felt . . . lost."

"Was Brian your only friend?"

"Pretty much," he admitted.

She laughed. "Don't worry. My only friend was a dragon."

Suddenly, Dree's smile disappeared. A shadow of concern fell over her face.

"Lourdvang's okay in Dracone," Marcus said. "I'm sure of it."

"I know," Dree said, though her voice betrayed her fear. "I just want to get back and help."

"Just one more day," Marcus said, as George walked ahead checking the night sky for drones. "We'll go for the Egg tomorrow night right at sundown. George said so."

"You mean your dad?" Dree asked softly.

Marcus paused. "Yeah, my . . . I'm not sure I'm ready to call him that yet."

Dree stepped up beside him, watching as George waved them forward. "You don't think he's telling the truth about Francis? That he was forced to build the drones?"

"I just think he still has a lot to answer for."

"We're here," George called back.

Marcus hurried up beside him and frowned. "Where?"

George smiled and pointed at a burger joint with a blinking neon sign. "Underneath."

Marcus laughed in disbelief. "The CIA annex is in Johnny Burger?"

Johnny Burger was Brian's absolute favorite restaurant. He and Marcus had eaten there for years. Johnny called them the "twin terrors" because of how many fries they could devour, and Marcus suspected that he and Brian were the reason Johnny eventually ended all-you-can-eat Thursdays.

"You know it?" George asked.

"You could say that," Marcus said. "So where's the entrance?"

"It all looks the same, actually," he said. "Okay, listen. There should be a dumpster out back. There will be a camera hidden in the tree behind it, and another set into the roof. There should be two doors on the back of the building . . . one will have no handle and should have a MAINTENANCE sign on it. Check and see if there is a little square groove next to it—seamless and black. If there is, then I know the first security measure hasn't changed. It's just a fingerprint scanner. Check it out and get back here."

"You're not coming?" Dree asked.

George laughed. "It would cause a lot of trouble if I popped up on there. Just act like two kids sneaking around to hang out or something. Do not make it obvious. Just try to be casual back there."

"Why would the two of us just be walking around back where it's dark and—" Marcus paused. "Never mind."

Dree rolled her eyes and started for the burger joint. "Let's go."

They pretended to stroll around the back of the squat, brown building into a small loading area with a rusted green dumpster that smelled like old potatoes and malt. Marcus started whistling and casually took Dree's hand, feeling the heat prickling through his skin at the touch. Dree just looked at him and shook her head.

"You're terrible at this."

"Spying or acting like we're a couple?"

"Both."

She pulled him into a hug, and this time the tingles raced through his entire body. It felt like he'd be electrocuted, and even Dree gasped a little at the sudden flood of heat. "Turn us toward the wall."

Marcus did as he was told.

"And?" she asked.

Marcus looked around. A slate-gray door labeled MAINTENANCE was set into the wall, although there was clearly a separate entrance for the employees, with Johnny's logo. Marcus had never really noticed the door before, even though they had hung out behind the burger joint at least a hundred times. It was hard to concentrate with the tingles running through him, but he examined the roofline for cameras.

"There is still one on the roof," he said quietly.

"One on the tree too," she said. "And on the fence."

"That's a new one," he murmured. He spotted a little square groove by the door. "I see the fingerprint scanner too. Looks like everything is in order. Are you ready to—"

He was cut off as the gray door suddenly slid open. A woman with a severe ponytail and a crisp black suit stepped out and then frowned when she saw them. Marcus saw the bulge of a gun at her hip.

"What are you doing here?" she asked.

Dree pulled Marcus in even closer, pressing their cheeks together like they were kissing.

Then she pulled away, looking shyly nervous. "Sorry . . . just with my boyfriend."

The woman snorted as the door slid shut behind her and then started for the parking lot.

"You might want to find somewhere a little more private. Not to mention it's late. Both of you should be at home studying. If I was your mom I would be dragging you back by your ears, trust me."

She disappeared around the front, and Dree turned to Marcus, smiling awkwardly. "That was a close call."

"Yeah," he said, shifting.

She suddenly let go of him. "We should probably go report to your dad . . ."

"I agree," Marcus replied. "He'll be glad to know about that fence camera."

"For sure," Dree said, patting his arm and then grimacing. "Okay then."

They hurried back to George, not talking. Marcus's cheeks were still burning brightly.

"Everything like I said?" George asked. "Are you guys all right? I saw the agent come out."

"Fine," Marcus said. "Everything is good. One extra camera. All good."

"What did you say to her?" he asked, frowning.

Marcus and Dree exchanged an awkward look. "Not much," Dree murmured.

George just laughed and shook his head. "Fair enough. Well, we can deal with one extra camera, I think. Let's get back. We could all use some sleep tonight. We have a *very* long day tomorrow."

A woman sat on a golden comet, streaking across the sky. Her hair shone like the morning light, and as Marcus watched, she flew closer—close enough that he could see the comet was a dragon. The woman had a gleaming silver sword slung over her back, and familiar blue eyes—his eyes. He knew this woman.

He could feel love and warmth as she smiled at him, growing ever closer.

"Hello, my son," she said in a clear voice, though she still seemed so far away.

He reached out for her, trying to take her hand.

But then a shadow fell over him, sweeping the entire land into darkness. He looked up and saw a massive red shape soar overhead, his fell wings spanning miles, if not forever. Helvath the chieftain.

Marcus screamed out a warning, but he was too late. Helvath blew a great wave of fire, swallowing the Rider and her dragon, and then all that was left were flames.

But then he looked down and saw that the fire was coming from him.

"Marcus!" The voice was loud and urgent.

Marcus's eyes shot open, and he sat up, feeling sweat pouring down his face. His father was sitting beside him, just barely visible in the moonlight seeping in through the curtains. He looked concerned.

"I heard you talking in your sleep," George said.

"Oh," Marcus murmured. "Sorry I woke you."

He had offered Dree his old bedroom, but she said she preferred the couch.

"I don't sleep much," George offered. "Consequence of sitting in a chair for the last few years, I guess." He searched Marcus's face, as if waiting for him to open up. After a long moment of silence, George pressed on. "Were you having a nightmare?"

"Yeah."

"Do you want to talk about it?"

"Um . . . I think it was about Mom."

George was silent for a moment, then climbed to his feet. He paced around the room.

"I always thought about what your bedroom might look like," he said. "I wondered if you had posters. Or medals if you were an athlete, or maybe stacks of books if you were a writer. I should have known you'd end up a scientist."

He picked up a plaque from one of Marcus's shelves. "An award-winning scientist, it would seem."

"I just won a couple of things," Marcus muttered.

George laughed. "State Science Fair Champion for three years in a row? I'd say that's pretty darn impressive." He sighed deeply and turned to the window. The curtains were drawn shut. "I wish I could have been there, Marcus."

"Yeah, I know. But you were sort of preoccupied."

"Yes," George responded, his voice suddenly softer, sadder. "But you're all I thought about. You, and your mother."

Marcus watched him, a frail silhouette against the moonlight. He had a million questions for his father, but only one came to mind in this moment. "What was she like?"

He opened his mouth to speak and then shook his head. "Maybe when this is over, Marcus. It's painful to talk about her. When the war is done, you and I can go over everything."

He turned to Marcus and smiled sadly.

"Just know that you and your mom have always been the most important things in the world to me."

Marcus allowed himself just a little flicker of resentment. "I thought the most important thing to you was becoming a Rider."

George sighed. "Not the most important, no, but it was my greatest sin. Injured pride, I guess. I don't know. I admit I led all us down this road, and for that I am sorry. For everything, really. I'm sorry."

Marcus didn't know what to say, so he just let the silence hold.

George smiled. "Get some sleep. Tomorrow we go after the Egg."

He went out to the living room, and Marcus lay back down, thinking about how one decision had changed all of their lives. But did it mean his father was a bad person? Did he deserve a second chance?

Marcus shook his head and rolled over. It didn't really matter at the moment.

First they had a war to win.

Marcus had just dozed off when he heard it: *Bang. Bang. Bang.*

Marcus jumped out of bed, his eyes locked on the far wall. Outside his fifth-story window, something was banging on the glass. He stood up and slowly walked toward the window, the noise continuing like a beating war drum. He felt his whole body tremble.

In one swift motion, Marcus pushed aside the curtain, then quickly ducked out of the way. But nothing was there. Slowly, Marcus slid the glass pane open.

Suddenly, something burst in through the opening, sending Marcus flying backward.

Chapter 4

Marcus slammed into the hardwood floor, his head connecting with a *thud*. As he tried to scramble to his feet, the little black object made its way to the desk, and Marcus realized that it must be after something. Did Francis think they had already stolen the Egg? Had he sent a drone to try to retrieve it? Or was this the CIA?

Marcus was about to call for help when the object suddenly stopped, hovered for a moment, and then lowered itself onto the desk.

Marcus's exhausted brain finally clicked into place. "*Bug?*" he asked incredulously.

He hurried over and tenderly picked up the little drone, which was covered in dirt and even had a little dandelion sprouting off its black hull. Marcus had flicked on Lightning Bug's transmitter when they arrived at the apartment, but he never actually expected the drone to return. Before landing in Dracone, Marcus had spent months building Lightning Bug, a small Researcher drone that he used to find the portal. When Marcus was swept up in the storm, he assumed Bug had been destroyed. He hugged the drone to his chest, surprised and relieved to have it back.

"I can't believe you're all right, buddy," he said, inspecting the drone for damage.

There was a quick knock at the door.

"Come in," Marcus said.

Dree stepped inside, rubbing her eyes. "I heard a noise." She stopped. "Is that—"

"Don't worry," Marcus said. "I made this one. Dree, meet Lightning Bug. Bug, say hello."

The drone beeped and began to fly toward Dree, who immediately stepped back. "I don't exactly like drones, remember?"

"Bug is different," Marcus said. "He's not dangerous. He just chases storms and collects data for me."

Dree cast a suspicious glance toward Bug, then looked around Marcus's bedroom. "It's like a laboratory in here," she said.

Marcus laughed. "Yeah, I was real popular." He placed Bug down on his desk, stroking the drone's metal casing affectionately. "Can't sleep either?" he asked Dree. "That seems to be a theme here tonight."

"I was sleeping just fine," she said pointedly, eyeing Lightning Bug again. "But I *am* getting restless. I'm glad we're finally going after the Egg tomorrow night—I can't stand waiting around anymore."

"But Earth's not so terrible, is it?" Marcus asked, feeling a bit protective of his home.

Dree smiled. "Well, I do like your burgers here. We need those in Dracone."

"*Definitely*," Marcus said, grinning. "We'll start a burger shop after the war. Dree's Dragon Burgers."

Dree raised her eyebrows.

"Oh, right," Marcus said, thinking about the wording. "I didn't mean . . . they won't, like, be *made* of dragons. How about Driele's Hand-Fried Hamburgers? Cooked on her actual hands!"

"No. And don't call me Driele either," she said, trying not to smile. "Anyway, I don't think I can open a burger shop with you. I'll be too busy as a Dragon Rider."

Marcus sat down beside her. "True. So that's the plan? Become a Dragon Rider? Fly around Dracone and protect the people and keep the peace and all that?"

"It's what I was born for. And so were you, remember?"

"I know. It's just . . . a different career path. Awesome . . . but different." Marcus paused and then looked down at his hands. "What about the whole . . . fire thing?"

"My dad never really explained it to me," Dree said. "But I did overhear him talking about me to another former Rider once. It was years ago, before his injury, when he was leading the Resistance group that was getting suspicious of Francis Xidorne. It was late, and I was supposed to be in bed, but I heard my name so I listened from the hallway. They talked about *Furies*."

"What's that?"

"Special Riders. I couldn't hear everything, and the woman he was talking to was even quieter, but I definitely heard him say something about *living fire*. They could create and control fire. They were also exceptionally rare, but whenever they arrived, they changed Dracone forever."

"And you think we're Furies?" Marcus asked.

"I don't know. But it makes sense. When does your fire come out?"

"When I'm angry or upset. Just ask my Xbox. So yeah . . . the name makes sense. But is it . . . a good thing to be a Fury? Changing Dracone forever sounds a little . . . vague."

Dree sighed. "I don't know. I guess we'll find out more when we get home."

"Still sounds funny," Marcus mused. "Talking about going home when I'm sitting in my bedroom."

Dree smiled, though she looked troubled for a moment. And then she stood up, stretching and looking down at the little black drone sitting next to Marcus.

"Are you going to bring Bug back to Dracone?"

Marcus stared at the little drone, thinking.

"Actually, I think we may have a job for him."

"I still can't believe you built this guy," George said proudly, fitting LB with a brand new transmitter.

Marcus watched in amazement as his dad worked. Marcus had always been good with technology, but his father was a wizard. His slender, almost skeletal hands flew over the wiring even as he programmed the upgrades on the laptop simultaneously. His eyes flicked from one machine to the other, never stopping for long.

"Jack gave me all the tools," Marcus said. "He helped with the concept design too. He was always encouraging me to work on new designs."

At the mention of Jack, a fresh wave of guilt swept through Marcus. Where was his uncle? Was he okay? George didn't seem too concerned, but Marcus wasn't so sure. What if Jack hadn't gotten away in time? What if the CIA had him? Or worse, what if Francis had gotten to him? Marcus shuddered to think of Francis interrogating his uncle. He could use him to build more drones.

"So what is this thing going to do again?" Dree asked, standing by the window. She had been doing that all day now, sometimes pacing with her hands clenched at her sides. He knew she was growing restless.

"Bug is going to fly up to each of the surveillance cameras outside of Johnny Burger and transmit a signal," Marcus said. "That signal is going to loop their feeds, so they see the same thing constantly even as we walk up to the door. Cool, right?"

Dree wandered back over, her interest obviously piqued. "Huh. Helpful little device. Well, that gets us through one obstacle."

George finished with the transmitter and sat back, nodding. "Yes, but not the other. The fingerprint scanner."

"So the entrance is just fingerprint protected?" Marcus asked.

"Fingerprint *and* password protected," George said, sighing. "And I don't have either one."

"But Jack is cleared for the annex, right?"

George glanced at him. "Yes, but without access to him—"

Marcus stood up, interrupting George. "We're going to have to do without. I can guess Jack's password—I know most of the ones for his computers and credit cards and stuff."

"And the fingerprints?" Dree asked.

Marcus looked around the apartment. "We're surrounded by them!"

George's face lit up. "*Of course*," he said. "We can lift a fingerprint from the house. We just need—"

"Hair gel," Marcus finished, smiling at his father. "I know. Jack taught me well."

George smiled, but a sadness suddenly filled his eyes. There was no time to discuss, though.

They had to get moving.

Marcus carefully slid the knife under a clump of hair gel and then pulled it out, grinning. Dree and George were both watching over his shoulder, which was making him very nervous, but he managed to lay the knife down with ease. Then he took a blow dryer, set it to the very lowest level, and started to dry the gel.

"Very clever," George mused.

The gel was already hardening, and Marcus could clearly see the grooves of Jack's fingerprints on the knife. It was far from a guarantee that the fingerprint would be clear enough for the scanner, but it gave them a chance—to get into the annex, at least. After that, George could only guess at what they would face.

The pomade grew rigid, and Marcus tenderly picked it up, examining the fingerprint.

"This might just work—"

He was cut off by a sharp knock at the door. He jumped and dropped the fingerprint, grabbing at it as it floated down and onto the floor. Dree was up in a second, snatching the knife and stalking toward the door.

Still clutching the knife, she looked through the peephole and relaxed. "Your friend."

She opened it and Brian strode in, flushing instantly when he saw Dree.

"Hello, Dree," he said, his eyes darting to her hand. "Is that . . . a steak knife?"

Dree tucked the knife behind her. "Sorry."

"No problem," he said, plopping down next to Marcus as he retrieved the imprint and put it back on the table, scowling. "Oh," Brian said. "A gel imprint? Very cool. So you're like a spy now too?"

Marcus shrugged. "More like a thief. And what are you doing here?"

"Well, I know you told me to go home—"

"Yes," George said.

"But," he continued, ignoring the comment, "I thought I should come by just to be sure you don't need my help." He held up the bag of fast food. "Anyone?"

Dree appeared in a flash, grabbing a burger and taking a huge bite out of it.

"Someone likes burgers," Brian said, watching her wolf it down. "There's this place, Johnny's—"

Marcus laughed. "Maybe another time."

"Fine," he said. "So . . . anything I can do? You can, like, lower me from a wire or something."

Marcus snorted. "That's just what I think of when I look at you. No . . . we're all right . . ."

"Actually," George said. "Maybe we *could* use you."

Marcus, Dree, and Brian all turned to him. "Really?" they all asked.

He nodded. "You can't get in the emergency exit . . . but you can knock on it."

"A distraction," Marcus said, turning to Brian. "Now that might work."

Brian's grin slowly slipped away. "Is this going to be dangerous?"

Marcus turned to the window, where the sun was already in the west. "Definitely."

Later that night, Marcus, Dree, and George once again crept through the Arlington cityscape, moving as quickly as they could. George was in the lead, with Dree close behind and Marcus at the tail. Lightning Bug floated along overhead, scanning the sky for other drones. Marcus could see his creation darting along and around buildings, but as of yet it hadn't spotted anything. No red eyes blazing in the darkness, no humming sound of a hovering Destroyer. For now, at least, they seemed to be in the clear.

"We're here," George said, as they stopped in an alley across from Johnny Burger.

Marcus and Dree joined him, and then Marcus looked up at Bug. "Go!"

The small drone zoomed past them, hovering above each surveillance camera in turn to transmit a code that would loop their current recording. It stopped at the last camera above the door, and then beeped twice to indicate that the signal had been successfully transmitted. All three cameras would now show the same empty parking lot on a loop. Meanwhile, Brian was trying to force his way into the other door down the block, and hopefully the agents were heading there now. George guessed that they would just tell him off and send him on his way. Marcus hoped he was right.

"Excellent," George said, watching as Bug hovered in the middle of the parking lot, as if waiting for them. "Very advanced design, Marcus."

Marcus flushed a little. "Yeah. I mean, Jack got the parts. But yeah . . . I built it."

"That's my boy."

They hurried over to the innocuous metal door, and Marcus turned to Bug.

"Go wait for us at home, okay, buddy? Good work."

The small drone took off, and George stepped up to the metal door, took a quick look in either direction, and nodded to Marcus.

"Here goes nothing," he muttered.

Marcus took a deep breath and stepped forward. He withdrew the replica he had made of Jack's fingerprint in the hair gel, handling it very carefully. Marcus placed the thin, waxy replica on the scanner, pressing it firmly to make sure it could read the fine imprint.

Sure enough, the door slid open, revealing a small lobby with an elevator.

"Nice," Dree said. "Maybe *you* should be a spy."

"He takes after his old man," George added, leading them into the elevator.

Marcus flushed. He felt strangely pleased, though he wasn't quite ready to think of George as his "old man."

"Round two," he said, eyeing the keypad beside the elevator.

He tried to hide his disappointment. The keypad had numbers *and* letters. Jack's password could be almost anything. He tried Jack's debit pin, then his birthday, then his street name. He tried Jack's mom's name (Carol), his first pet (Ralphie), his favorite number (14)—nothing was working.

Marcus shook his head, defeated. "I'm sorry, guys . . . I don't know. I thought I'd be able to figure this out, but—"

"What about *Marcus*?" George cut in.

Marcus looked at him. "What?"

"He raised you like a son," George said, his voice gentle. "You're the biggest part of his life. Try typing in *Marcus*."

Marcus punched in his name. The door slid open.

"Oh," he whispered.

George patted Marcus's shoulder. "Come on, let's go."

Marcus flushed yet again. He had kind of always assumed that Jack just put up with him because he had to. Jack didn't really show any affection either. This was strangely touching. Marcus stepped inside the elevator and saw that there was only one floor below them, just as George had described.

George turned to them. "Now it gets tricky. Ready?"

They both nodded, and he hit the button.

"They will be alerted that the elevator is moving, so we have to be quick." He put another tiny round transmitter on the elevator controls and flicked it on just as the doors opened. "Follow me!"

They ran out of the elevator and turned right into a

small office that Marcus remembered from the plans that George had drawn out back at the apartment. The entire annex was painted a sterile white, like a creepy hospital basement, and smelled like floor cleaner and recycled air. Dree carefully closed the office door behind them, and George ushered them behind a large desk. "Stay out of sight," he whispered.

Footsteps came storming down the hall, and Marcus held his breath as he heard a voice on the other side of the door . . .

"Lisa, come in," a man was saying. "The elevator just came down. It's empty."

A loud voice came crackling back over a walkie-talkie. "I'm almost to the other door. It's just some kid messing around. I'll tell him to get lost and be right back to help you look. You check the cameras?"

"Yeah. No one came in."

"The elevator must be malfunctioning. Why don't you take a quick look outside just to be sure?"

"Good idea," George murmured, as they heard footsteps getting farther and farther away. George pressed his ear up to the door. "The elevator doors just closed. We'll let it get halfway up and then—"

He pressed a button on his little pocket transmitter and grinned. Through the door, they could hear the elevator as it squeaked to a stop between floors. "Voilà! He's stuck in the elevator. Let's move . . ."

George opened the door and was about to exit when Dree grabbed his arm and yanked him back inside. "*Wait,*" she whispered. "There's still someone out there."

They all froze, and soon they could hear the man's voice again.

"I sent it back up," the agent said into his walkie-talkie, "to see if it was malfunctioning. I think it just got stuck."

"So just a broken elevator, then," Lisa replied. "Better call the head office."

Still ducking under the desk, George frowned. "Well, that's not good." He looked around the room, and his eyes fell on a laptop. "Plan B." He scooped the laptop off the table and sat down with it, his fingers flying over the keyboard.

"What are you doing?" Marcus whispered.

"I set up this security system with Jack," he murmured. "I always build in overrides."

An alarm suddenly went off in another area of the annex, and they heard the man curse and take off down the hall. "Another alarm just went off!" he shouted into the walkie-talkie. "You better get back here!"

"Quickly now," George said, climbing to his feet.

Marcus and Dree hurried after George as he eased out the door, waiting for the guard to turn down the hallway. Then he started to briskly walk in the same direction, Dree and Marcus close behind.

"He'll only take a minute or two to turn off the alarm," George said. "Faster."

They were almost at a full run when a muffled voice filtered through the noise.

"Marcus?"

They all slid to a stop. Marcus ran up to one of the doors lining the hallway, where a small glass window revealed a familiar face: Uncle Jack was staring back at him. Marcus pressed the automatic lock and Jack hurried out, looking at Marcus incredulously. And then he saw George.

"You're back," he whispered.

The two men embraced, and then Jack stepped back and looked between him and Marcus.

"Finally," he said, grinning.

"What are you doing here?" Marcus asked.

"The CIA started looking for your father again. I'm guessing when Marcus went through the portal, he triggered another electromagnetic disturbance . . . just like George did. They must have picked it up. They took me in for questioning a week ago. I told them nothing, but the agency is still looking for you, George. If they find you in here, they'll lock us *all* up in here."

"We're here for the Egg," George said.

Recognition filled Jack's eyes. "Let's move."

"*Freeze!*" a commanding voice shouted from down the hall.

The guard was walking toward them, his gun pointed right at Jack's forehead.

"Nobody move or I open fire."

Chapter 5

Dree watched as the armed man stalked toward them, his index finger quivering over the trigger. The man was tall and lean, but he clearly wasn't a warrior. His pale face was flushed and sweating. He had probably never expected any trouble at this secret annex.

Marcus, George, and Jack all had their hands raised, and Dree knew that if they were detained, the mission was over. The Egg would stay where it was, and Francis Xidorne would win.

That was not an option.

"Sorry," she murmured. But she wasn't saying it to the guard.

Dree raised her hands, letting her fingers brush against Marcus's T-shirt. As she released all of the anger and frustration and fear of the last few weeks, rippling flames leapt from her fingertips and quickly caught on Marcus's shirt. Fire raced up his back, and George shouted in alarm, immediately working to pat out the fire. Marcus, who hadn't even noticed the heat, saw the commotion and knew what to do next. He flailed and screamed, pretending to burn terribly. It was quite a show.

The CIA agent hesitated, but soon hurried forward, trying to help.

That's when Dree made her move. She cocked her fist and punched the man across the jaw, dropping him hard to the sterile white floor. His gun went clattering down the hall. Dree rubbed her knuckles gingerly and turned to the other three, who were staring at her, stunned. The fire was out, and Marcus grinned.

"Not bad," he said.

"I try."

George looked between them, his eyes scanning over Marcus's charred shirt. "It didn't . . . why didn't it hurt you?"

Marcus forced a smile. "We're both immune to the fire."

George narrowed his eyes. "Are you sure?"

"Pretty sure," Marcus replied, shrugging.

George was silent for a moment, and then he shook his head. "We need to get the Egg. We don't have long before the other agents arrive. Soon, this whole place will be locked down. Follow me."

They ran down the hallway to another elevator door—this one at the far end of the annex. Jack led them inside and punched in a short code. The elevator jumped and started the descent.

"How did you get in?" Jack asked.

"Turns out you raised our boy well," George responded. Jack glanced at Marcus proudly.

"The lower level is deep below the surface," George explained. "It's where the research floor is located, and it's where I built the vault." He cast a worried glance at Marcus. "We don't have long. I predict five minutes until reinforcements arrive and get the first elevator working. We'll need to move—"

He was cut off as the elevator suddenly lurched to a halt, causing them all to stumble. Dree caught herself on the wall as a piercing alarm split through the air, filling the elevator like the dragon sirens back in Dracone.

George paused. "Perhaps I miscalculated."

"What now?" Marcus asked frantically.

Jack looked around the elevator, and then turned to Dree. "Boost me up."

Dree didn't stop to think—she just put her hands together. Jack stepped onto them and reached up for the ceiling. She lifted and he slid one of the ceiling panels aside. "We're going to have to climb down."

Marcus blanched. "Climb down the pulley cable?"

He nodded. "It's the only way. One more push, please."

Dree heaved, and Jack pulled himself up through the

ceiling before reaching back down for the rest of them. One by one they pulled themselves out, until they were all perched atop the elevator like a flock of pigeons. The only pale light filtered up from the inside of the elevator. Dree took a quick peek over the edge and saw nothing but darkness. They would be descending completely blind.

Tentatively, Jack reached out and grabbed the cable. "Here goes nothing," he muttered.

He stepped out over the side, still clutching the cable, and started climbing down.

"Are you sure you can do this?" Marcus asked his father, who was still frail from his time in Dracone.

George nodded grimly. "I think so."

He started after Jack, leaving Marcus and Dree alone. She squeezed Marcus's hand.

"He'll be fine. *We'll* be fine."

Marcus snorted. "We'll see. I wasn't exactly the best in gym. You want to go first?"

She shook her head. "I'll be right behind you."

Marcus slowly started down the pulley, and then Dree reached out and caught the hard cable, gripping it with both hands. She stepped out over the chasm, feeling her stomach flop and roll over as she shifted her entire weight onto her arms, leaving solid ground behind her. Flying on Lourdvang was one thing, but this blind descent into an abyss did not appeal to her at all. Trying not to look down, she started climbing hand over hand, wrapping her legs around the cable just in case her fingers slipped.

"Okay?" Jack called out from the bottom.

"Super," Marcus managed, his strained voice echoing in the elevator shaft.

The climb seemed to take forever. Dree didn't even see the floor until her hide boots scraped the concrete. The other three were standing next to her, peering out into a flashing hallway. She removed her aching hands and hurried up behind them.

"Let's go," George said. The alarm was still blaring. "The alternate exit is at the far end of the hallway . . . it leads to the exterior door where your friend Brian was trying to get in. We grab the Egg and make for that. We have to be fast. If you get separated, remember there is a second small exit that leads out of a sewer grate. Both of them can only be *exited*, but we can use them now."

He ran down the hall, and Dree followed in the rear, blinking against the flashing white lights that lined the walls and cringing as the alarm grew ever louder. They passed a few closed metal doors, and she wondered just what Jack and George had been experimenting on down here. Were there half-built drones just sitting behind those doors in the darkness? She shuddered just thinking about the glowing red eyes.

George slid to a halt in front of a slate door. It looked almost impenetrable.

"This one never changed," Jack said softly.

George keyed in a code, and Marcus, eyeing the numbers, turned to his father.

"What was the password?"

His father glanced at him and then turned back as the door slid open. "Eria."

The vault was no bigger than a closet. A glass case stood upon a raised stoned platform, and sitting in the middle of the glass case was an ebony egg, as black as tar and a bit larger than a soccer ball. Red and orange ripples moved across the black surface like waves, and Dree felt the little hairs on her arms stand up. The Egg had a tangible, almost visceral energy that she felt all the way down to her bones. Dragon magic.

George noticed everyone's awestruck expressions. "Now you see why I desired it so much," he said.

He was reaching to remove the case when a shout burst through the air.

"Step away from that case!" a woman ordered.

Dree glanced down the hall and realized that the other agent had returned. They had all been so transfixed by the Egg that they hadn't noticed her stepping into the hall, gun raised.

She looked angry.

Jack turned to her. "Listen, Lisa, just—"

She didn't wait. She fired a warning shot well wide of them, the bullet chewing into the rock.

"Run!" George said.

They took off down the hallway, and the agent sprinted after them, clearly not willing to gun them down just yet.

Dree pulled ahead, her eyes on the door at the end of the hallway. Their escape route.

But the agent was closing in fast, and Dree knew that by the time they opened that door, the agent would be on top of them. They were trapped.

George must have realized the same thing, because he suddenly stopped and turned back to the agent.

"Dad!" Marcus shouted. "What are you doing?"

Jack and Dree slowed down, grabbing for Marcus's arm.

George turned and looked at his son.

"Go," he said firmly. "Remember. If you can weather the storm—"

Marcus shook his head. "No, Dad—"

"Marcus, if you can weather the storm, home—"

"Home is on the other side," Marcus finished softly, the two of them locking eyes as the CIA agent slammed into George, tackling him to the ground.

The group fled to the end of the hall, and Dree pulled the door open, gesturing for Jack and Marcus to run.

"Go!" she screamed.

Marcus and Jack burst through the door and sprinted down the corridor. Dree watched them go before turning back to the hallway, where the agent was pinning George.

They were still at war, and Dree wasn't going back empty-handed.

Chapter 6

Marcus felt his legs moving, but he didn't even know who was controlling them. All he could think of was his father, pinned to the concrete floor, smiling as Marcus and the others got away. Tears streamed down Marcus's cheeks, but he barely felt those either. After all these years, after so much searching, he had lost his father again. And they didn't even retrieve the Egg.

He had failed.

Jack slowed down, grasping his cramping sides. Neither had done a lot of exercising in their many years together, unless furiously typing code counted. The corridor was long and straight—built out of the rock and slate-gray metal.

White warning lights were flashing on the walls, making everything look dreamlike and surreal.

"What now?" Jack gasped, taking off his glasses and wiping his sweaty forehead.

Marcus shook his head. "Should we go back?"

He turned to see what Dree thought, but she wasn't behind him. The hallway stretched back to the annex, bathed in flickering light. But no one else was there. Dree was gone.

"She was right behind us," Jack said, panic creeping into his voice.

"I'm going back," Marcus said immediately, turning around.

He had only taken a few steps when a massive steel door slid shut, blocking the way back to the annex. Marcus yelped and jumped back, stunned. Dree was trapped inside the building.

"The other agent must have woken up," Jack said, grabbing Marcus's shoulder and pulling him back toward the exit. "He's locked down the annex. We can't go back now."

"But—"

"Marcus, we can't be here right now. We'll figure out a way to get them back. *Both* of them. But we can't help if we're caught too."

"I won't leave her," Marcus said, a bit more sharply than he had intended.

Jack met Marcus's eyes. "We don't have a choice. And for all we know, she might have made it out somewhere else.

We have to trust that your friend can take care of herself. At least for now."

More than anything, Marcus wanted to head back into the annex, but he knew his uncle was right. He nodded, and they continued down the hall, the white lights flashing furiously around them. They stumbled on down the seemingly endless corridor, and only then did Marcus see one of the storm doors begin to close ahead of them. They were trapped.

"Hurry!" Jack said, breaking into a sprint.

Marcus ran after him, moving faster than he ever had in his life. His sneakers pounded off the concrete, and Jack threw himself through the door headfirst. It was nearly closed. Marcus lunged forward, twisting himself in midair to fit through the narrowing gap. His sneakers cleared the door by mere inches, and he crashed into the unforgiving concrete with a bone-crushing thud. His right shoulder screamed with pain, wrenching sideways beneath him, and he grimaced as Jack pulled him to his feet.

"We're out," Jack said, pointing to some stairs just ahead of them.

He led Marcus up the steps, and they emerged through another hidden door behind a seedy strip mall. When it closed, he saw there was no door handle or controls on the other side. Marcus grabbed his right shoulder as they ran out into the empty parking lot—it was aching terribly.

"Where's the other exit?" he demanded. "We need to check it for Dree."

"It's too dangerous," Jack argued.

"Show me."

Jack sighed and then started jogging back toward the burger joint where they had first entered.

"There is a little grate close by," he said, looking around. "There it is."

He led Marcus to another empty parking lot behind a hardware store, and Marcus spotted a grate tucked into the brick on the other side. It was old and rusted, with a strange lock covered in grime.

"Just a quick look," Jack said, checking the street. "They'll swarm the entire area soon."

Marcus was just starting for the grate when it was flung open. Dree emerged, her pack slung over her shoulders. Marcus grinned. He should have known Dree wouldn't be captured that easily. He waved to get her attention, and she turned to him, catching his eye.

Then she turned away and started running.

"Hey!" Marcus shouted, "Dree, where are you going?"

She didn't answer. Instead, Marcus watched as she jumped over a fence and sprinted away. She was leaving them behind.

Marcus ran after her.

"Marcus . . . wait!" Jack shouted.

Marcus ignored him. How could Dree just leave him now, after everything they had been through? Was she going back to Dracone alone?

It didn't make any sense.

Jack was close behind him, and Marcus leapt over the fence, catching a glimpse of Dree down the alley. She was faster than him, but she was out of her element—she didn't know Arlington. Marcus took a shortcut down the other side of the building, and as he rounded the wall onto the street, he ran right into Dree. Marcus grabbed her arm, and she tried to yank it away, but he held on firmly, turning her to face him.

"You have to stay," she pleaded, trying to get her arm free.

Marcus frowned. "What are you talking about?"

Jack rounded the corner behind them before doubling over, gasping.

Dree's shoulders slumped, defeated. "You can't lose him again, Marcus," she said quietly. "He's your family. You've done a lot for Dracone, but it's not your problem anymore. You *just* found your dad. You can't leave him like this. You have to go back."

Marcus saw the pain in her eyes, and he realized she was thinking of her own father too. She had told Marcus a lot about how he had slipped away after his injury, leaving a shell behind. It had felt like Dree had lost a little bit more of her father with every passing day. And she knew how much Marcus had wanted to find his father—how it had consumed him for years and led him all the way to war in Dracone. But he was a part of that war now, and he had to stop it. He couldn't just leave her. He took her hand, meeting her eyes.

"Thank you," he said hoarsely. "But I have to go back. It's my home too, remember?"

"Marcus—"

"I'm a part of this, Dree. My dad . . . he is the cause of this war. And I know he would want me to deal with Francis first. He would want me to go back. I'm not going to leave you, okay?"

Dree nodded, and for just a second he thought he caught a hint of tears in her eyes.

"Okay," she said softly. "We'll do it together."

"It's our only chance," Marcus replied.

"I agree," Jack said, straightening up again. "But we can't go to this Dracone yet. We need to get the Egg."

Dree smiled. "No, we don't."

She reached into her pack and pulled out the Egg. It glinted red and orange in the darkness, rippling as if freshly pulled from a fire.

"You got it?" Marcus asked, amazed.

"That agent was a little preoccupied with your father," she said. "He managed to put up a fight long enough for me to grab the Egg and run for it. I couldn't help him escape, though. I'm sorry."

"He'll be okay," Jack said. "Let's get back to the apartment."

"They'll be watching it," Marcus warned. "We need to get to Dracone."

"I know," Jack said. "But we'll need my car if we're going to get out of the city."

61

They hurried through the night, hugging the walls and staying away from the main roads. Marcus and Dree constantly watched the skies, but the night was clear and starry. Perhaps the drones had never made it back to Earth after all.

When they reached the apartment, they watched it for a while, making sure it wasn't under surveillance. Satisfied, Jack ran to grab his keys, while Dree and Marcus waited in the underground parking lot. Jack returned a moment later, materializing in the dark. They piled into his old forest-green sedan, Marcus in the shotgun seat.

"We need to get to a field outside of the city," Marcus said, glancing at Jack. "I have the transmitter for the portal, but it's going to create a thunderstorm."

Jack nodded. "We'll head south. We don't have long. They'll be looking for this car."

He peeled out onto the road, and Marcus leaned back in his seat, rubbing his shoulder. He hoped he hadn't broken anything. It felt very tender, but he could still move it.

"So what happens when we get to Dracone?" Jack asked.

"We?" Marcus asked, glancing at him.

Jack looked at him. "Do you think I'm leaving you guys? No sir. I'm coming with you."

"It's going to be dangerous," Dree said from the back.

"And it's not here?" he countered. "I just escaped from the CIA. They're going to be after me. Hiding out in an alternate realm might not be the worst idea. Besides, with your dad detained, it's my job to keep you safe again. I let you go the first time . . . I'm not doing that again."

"Uncle Jack—"

"Don't bother," he cut in. "I'm coming. End of story. Now what happens when we get there?"

Marcus opened his mouth to argue but then just smiled instead. Even if he didn't want to admit it, he was kind of happy that Jack was coming. He couldn't wait to show him the dragons.

"We use the Egg to build a new hybrid," Dree replied. "And we go to war with the drones."

"Something to look forward to," Jack said sarcastically. "Marcus, how long does the portal take to form—"

"Oh no," Marcus whispered, cutting him off.

"What?" Dree asked.

Marcus peered out the windshield where a huge white shape was descending from the sky like a storm cloud, the moonlight reflecting off its angled wings and dual machine guns.

A Destroyer.

And it was coming right for them.

Chapter 7

"Impossible," Jack said, leaning forward to watch as the massive white drone swept down from the star-filled sky. "Our design—"

"It's real," Marcus cut in. "And it's about to blow us sky-high. Drive!"

Jack put his foot down, and Dree flew back into her seat as the car swerved onto a main road, causing several other drivers to slam on their brakes. Horns and angry shouts filled the air. Jack raced down the street, heading south as the outskirts of Arlington flashed past them in a blur. Dree rolled down her window and stuck her head out to get a better view, watching as the Destroyer drone made a ponderous turn, clearly following them. She could see the missiles protruding from beneath its wings, each one capable of turning their car into a smoking crater. But she had a feeling it wasn't going to destroy them just yet.

Francis Xidorne wanted the Egg—if he destroyed them, he destroyed the Egg too.

Dree clutched the bag to her chest. She would rather die than surrender it to Xidorne.

Jack swerved in and out of traffic, eliciting more horns and shouts. Marcus grabbed the armrest as they burst through a red light, and Dree shouted out a warning as a car just narrowly missed them.

"How many drones have been built?" Jack asked tersely, his eyes on the rearview mirror.

"We don't know," Dree said. "Francis has a factory in Dracone. He is building more every day. Fifty or more, I would guess."

"I can't believe it," Jack said, shaking his head. "Are there other kinds?"

Marcus nodded. "Trackers and Surveyors. They probably won't be far behind this one."

"Maybe it's time to start that thunderstorm?" Dree suggested as they raced around a truck. She cringed as they just narrowly avoided another onrushing vehicle. The driver shook his fist and honked.

"Agreed," Marcus said.

She watched him pull out the transmitter and punch in instructions, signaling the fixed transponders that George had placed throughout Arlington and Dracone. They created a huge web of energy disruptions, crisscrossing the area and merging the electrical frequencies of the two worlds. A massive storm would ensue, and the portal would open. If Francis didn't change his mind before then and have the Destroyer turn them into a smoking crater.

Marcus activated the transponders and then gazed upward. "It doesn't take long."

Already, the sky had begun to darken. The storm would erupt in minutes. They were heading into the outskirts now—suburban areas where the traffic was lighter. The drone decided to take advantage of that.

Dree shrieked a warning as the drone suddenly opened fire, targeting their tires. Jack wrenched the steering wheel to the right, and they all screamed as the car ran up onto the curb. A line of chewed-up pavement streaked past them as the bullets dug into the asphalt. Now everyone else had taken notice of the attack. Cars began to peel off the road, and Dree saw a pedestrian point and run just as the first sirens blared from somewhere close by. The police would be coming for them now.

The drone swept lower—maybe a hundred feet overhead—trying to get a better shot and blow out their tires. Dree turned back to the others. "Are there any weapons on this thing?"

"It's a Corolla," Jack said.

Dree looked at him, waiting.

"No!" he shouted, before veering out of the way of another burst of machine gun fire.

Outside, the sky grew darker and massive clouds were forming, obscuring the stars.

"How much farther?" Dree asked.

"Not much," Marcus said. "I directed the center of the storm at a clearing just south of here."

Another burst of machine gun fire tore into their bumper, ripping it from the car. Jack turned sharply, and Dree watched as the bumper clattered away behind them, surrounded by shooting sparks. There were more sirens in the air, and she saw the first white flashing car pull onto the road behind them.

"Perfect," Jack muttered.

A fork of lightning split the sky overhead. Marcus checked the transmitter.

"Almost ready," he said.

"Look out!" Dree screamed, pointing as a black Tracker emerged ahead of them, speeding down the road. The Tracker launched a missile, and Jack again turned sharply left, just narrowly avoiding it. But the missile was never aimed at them.

Dree watched in horror as it sped past them and hit the ground right in front of the police car. It exploded in a dramatic fireball, causing the cruiser to careen through the air and slam back into the road.

"They're trying to kill us!" Marcus shouted.

Dree shook her head. "They're making sure the cops don't capture us first."

"There!" Marcus said, pointing to a sprawling field that

opened up beside the road—stretching for a few miles at least. It was covered in knee-high grass and divots and ruts. The storm was raging fiercest there—lightning seemed to explode in the sky.

"Hold on!" Jack said.

Dree quickly put on her seat belt. "This is going to be bad."

Jack turned right and the car leapt off the shoulder, dropping a few feet onto the field. The car bounced horribly, causing Dree's head to slam into the ceiling as they sped across the grass. She gripped the pack tighter. They were almost there.

"It's not . . . exactly . . . an off-roader," Jack managed, trying to hold on to the wheel.

"Go left!" Dree shouted, as the Destroyer and Tracker both opened fire.

Jack turned, but he was just a bit too late. One of the bullets caught the back tire, and they heard a pronounced *thump* as it immediately went flat. The car started to list terribly to the right, and Jack struggled for control on the bumpy field. Marcus checked the readings again.

"The portal should be open soon," he said. "Head right for the middle of the storm—where the lightning is hitting the ground."

Jack looked at him. "We're going to drive into that lightning, aren't we?"

"Pretty much," Marcus said.

He steered them back and forth in a wild zigzag as both drones kept firing. Dree ducked as the back window was blown out. Glass sprayed over the inside of the car, and she covered her eyes.

"Faster!" she shouted.

"My foot is on the floor!" Jack shouted back.

The drones clearly didn't want to take any more chances. A missile flew past them and exploded into the ground ahead, chewing into the meadow and sending a plume of dirt flying in all directions. Jack steered around it, the flames racing over the car, and he shouted in alarm as the fire pressed in on them. Dree didn't even really notice the heat. The car buckled and jumped over the lip of the crater but kept moving.

"Can we drive through the portal?" Jack asked.

"I don't think so," Marcus said. "My bike didn't go through. You'll have to stop, and we'll run out."

"We won't have long before they cut us all down," Jack warned.

"We don't have a choice," Marcus countered, checking his transmitter. "Three . . . two . . . one . . . *now!*"

Jack slammed on the brakes, and Dree felt the seat belt dig into her chest. The car started to swerve across the grass, out of control with the flat tire, but the sudden stop had caught the drones by surprise. They flew directly overhead and wheeled in either direction, trying to turn back.

"Run!" Marcus said.

They piled out of the car, Dree tightly clutching the Egg, and they started sprinting to where the lightning was striking the ground again and again, smashing into the dirt and creating a mesmerizing pattern. The rain had started now, beating into their faces in a freezing sheet blown almost horizontal by the wind. Dree struggled to see as they dashed madly across the meadow. The drones had turned around, and they weren't waiting. Both started firing.

"Jump!" Marcus said, leaping forward and twisting himself to look back at Dree.

He disappeared in a flash of blue, Jack right behind him. Dree felt a cold bullet graze past her cheek, cutting into her skin. She cried out in pain as she threw her body toward the portal.

The world turned blue.

Chapter

8

Marcus groaned and rolled onto his back, lying sprawled out in the middle of a Draconian city street.

"We really need a better system," he said.

Dree pulled herself up beside him, helping Jack up as well. "Agreed."

There was a small trail of blood running down Dree's cheek from the bullet. She touched it and winced.

"You okay?" Marcus asked.

She nodded. "Just grazed me."

Marcus looked around as he stood up, massaging his sore shoulder. They were in the busy dragon market near the city center, lined with stalls and shoppers, and once again people seemed confused as they picked up their scattered, windblown possessions. Instead of newspapers and coffee cups, they were chasing after coiffed scarlet wigs, bizarre currency notes, and silken scarves. Many of the younger patrons were dressed in the new style: leather clothes and fire-resistant armor, shaved eyebrows, and necklaces, earrings, and rings of dragon teeth and scales. It was all a grim reminder of the dragon purge and the wave of terror that Francis Xidorne had unleashed.

People began to stare at them and mutter.

"We'd better go," Dree said, taking charge. Her eyes tracked the stalls darkly, though, and Marcus knew she was barely restraining her anger. Those stalls were selling the body parts of dragons.

The three of them started quickly down the worn cobblestone, heading deeper into the crowd. The Draconians looked curiously at Marcus and Jack and their unusual attire.

"Incredible," Jack whispered, staring at the strange city around them.

The drones weren't attacking these more affluent areas, and the homes and buildings of red brick and gray mortar loomed around them, while steel chimneys spouted smoke in the distance. Metal was slapped onto the buildings in the form of doors, window frames, or sometimes with no purpose at all other than to show the owner's wealth. Everything smelled of fire and ash.

"You haven't seen anything yet," Marcus said, thinking of Lourdvang and the other dragons.

Marcus was amazed by how . . . normal everything looked here. It was as if the residents weren't even aware of the war raging outside their city. People were simply milling about, talking and laughing in their fang necklaces and gleaming ebony armor—crimson-dyed hair shaved into elaborate patterns or Mohawks. The market stalls were lining the streets even here, busy as ever, and Marcus saw more dragon fangs and scales—the emerald green of Outliers, the black of Nightwings, and the rarer gold of Sages. As always, there was no crimson. The Flames were untouched. Marcus felt his skin crawl at the sight and saw Dree eyeing the booths again with her fists clenched, but he squeezed her arm.

"We have to keep a low profile," he reminded her.

The eastern mountains rose up before them, and Marcus knew that Dree's family would be hiding in the caves there, hopefully safe from danger. He checked the sky—the drones would begin searching for them soon. They had to leave the city immediately, before Francis could track them down.

"So this is where you were born," Jack said, glancing at Marcus.

Marcus nodded. "Apparently."

"Do these people even care about what's happening?" Dree said furiously, watching as a young couple walked past, laughing and holding hands.

"Easy," he said.

Dree nodded, obviously trying to control herself. But Marcus could see in her eyes that she was struggling to keep herself calm. He watched her hands start to clench, and little tendrils of fire began to dance over her skin, fiery red intermingled with orange and yellow and even a radiant blue. It moved like the currents in a stream, traveling up her fingertips and dissipating into the air. Her eyes flashed.

"Dree," he said, grabbing her arm gently. "Relax."

Jack was watching her now. And he wasn't alone. A few other people were glancing at her hands.

"I'm okay," Dree said, shoving her hands into her pockets. But her bare arms were still blazing.

Marcus looked ahead and saw that two soldiers were walking down the street in their direction, holding long spears propped over their shoulder and dressed in gleaming black armor. *Dragon armor.* It was the Protectorate—Francis's personal guard and warriors. And they were heading right for Dree, Marcus, and Jack.

"Come on," Marcus said, pushing Dree toward an alley.

As soon as they were out of view, they took a sharp left, emerging onto another busy street. Marcus risked a look back and saw that the guards had walked away. They had lost them for the moment.

"We need to get out of the city fast," Marcus said, eyeing Dree. "Keep it together, all right?"

"Fine," Dree murmured, looking away.

They hurried out of the downtown core and soon found themselves in the outskirts of Dracone. At the sight, Marcus felt his stomach drop into his feet, and stinging, acrid bile crept up his throat, threatening to come out. There was no longer any question whether or not a war was raging here. Ruins lined the streets—houses and shops were blown to pieces, leaving only piles of charred wood and blackened stone. Half-burned toys and clothes lay scattered everywhere like fallen leaves. Worse still, ashen survivors sat huddled in the ruins, sitting around small fires and draping rags over the protruding wooden beams like curtains. In some places Marcus saw bodies covered with white sheets or shrouded in the dust. Silence reigned, broken only once in a while by a shout or a baby's crying.

Marcus stopped, pressing his hand over his mouth. Dree was white as snow beside him.

"The drones did this?" Jack asked softly.

"Yes," Marcus said. "In many places. And they have killed countless dragons by now too."

Jack blanched, looking at another white-shrouded body. Marcus recognized the look on his face. He had been wearing the same one when he first came here. Guilt. Guilt for bringing the drones when he thought they had simply followed him back. And he still felt it eating away at his insides. Not guilt for anything he had done . . . he knew now that the drones had been tracking him *from* Dracone. This guilt was for his father. For bringing these terrible machines here in the first place.

"I . . . I never knew our invention might be used . . . for this," Jack managed, sounding faint.

"It wasn't the invention that did this," Marcus said. "It's the man who is using it."

"So much death," Jack said, still stunned.

"And that's why we have to stop him," Dree said, grabbing Marcus and leading him on.

They cut through the decimated streets, heading farther and farther out to where the houses had all been ramshackle wooden huts bordering the meadows. Now nothing was left but timber and ash. They passed a young woman sitting against a broken piece of wood. She glanced at them, and they saw that her face had been partially burned. Ash clouded her teeth.

"Hello," Dree said, crouching down beside her.

She nodded. "Good day."

Marcus saw two young kids sleeping on the ground, wrapped in threadbare blankets.

"When did this happen?" Marcus asked the woman.

She looked at him, and the blankness in her gray eyes struck him deeply.

"A week or two ago, I guess," she said, her voice faint. "I think, anyway. The machines came in the night. Destroyed the block. It was all screams and fire. I don't remember much."

Dree knelt down beside her. "They didn't give you any warning? No chance to run?"

She shook her head, and her knotted, filthy hair swayed over her gaunt cheeks. "No. We were asleep. This . . . this was our home."

She looked at the pile of charred logs, and her dull eyes started to water.

Dree squeezed the woman's hand. "We're going to make them pay for this."

The woman roughly wiped her eyes. "We can't fight those things," she said. "And we have nowhere to go. Nothing to eat but rats and whatever wild potatoes I can find in the meadow. The machines . . . they said it was the rebels controlling them. But the machines don't touch the city. They don't."

"They are controlled by Francis Xidorne," Dree said. "He is doing this to you."

She looked at Dree, frowning. "The Prime Minister?"

Dree nodded. "You can tell the others. Don't trust him. He will wipe you all out if he can."

She looked at Dree, and then at Marcus and Jack. "And you're . . . you're trying to stop him?"

"Yes," she said. "We're going to make him answer for all of this."

She forced a smile. "I hope you do, girl. But if you're fighting those machines, it's no use. Best run far away if you can."

Dree narrowed her eyes. "I won't hide from that monster. Take care of yourself. Take care of your children. We'll handle Xidorne."

Dree stood up again, and the three of them started for the mountains. Dree stormed ahead, fuming.

"You can't blame her for losing hope," Marcus said, catching up to Dree.

"No," Dree agreed coldly. "But we can save her."

Marcus nodded and looked toward the mountains. "Yes. But not alone."

When they finally reached the opening to the Nightwings' lair, Forost, all three were exhausted. It had taken almost a full day to get there, as they traveled through the lush green valleys before finally scaling the mountain. It was already dark, and the sky was covered with a tapestry of stars, unfettered by light pollution. It was cold, and Jack shivered at the icy wind that was howling across the mountains.

Dree led the group into Forost, and they immediately felt dragon heat wash over them. The main cavern bordering the entrance was mostly empty, expect for a few Nightwings perched together in shadowy corners, speaking in their low, growling language. Jack froze, staring at one of them.

"Oh, right," Marcus said, smiling. "These are dragons."

"I see that," Jack murmured. "I guess I didn't know what to expect."

"I still don't," Marcus agreed. "But we need to find Lourdvang—"

He was interrupted by an earsplitting roar that erupted in the cavern, causing Jack to stumble backward in surprise. Marcus turned to see Lourdvang racing across the chamber, almost at a full run. Dree shouted in delight and hugged his massive snout as he knelt down, nuzzling her.

Lourdvang snorted. "You took longer than you said you would," he said, black smoke curling from his nostrils.

"We ran into some . . . issues," Dree said.

The dragon stood up, towering over them. Marcus could just imagine what Jack was thinking. Lourdvang was about twenty feet tall, with great furled wings that could stretch out as long as a commercial jet. His skin was a shimmering ebony black, contrasted sharply by huge, icy-blue eyes.

But the most amazing thing about Lourdvang was the intelligence in his face—the expressive way that his eyes and mouth worked together, which was almost humanlike.

Marcus smiled up at him. "Hey, Lourdvang. This is my uncle Jack. He's here to help."

Jack's eyes widened as Lourdvang looked him over, exposing his gigantic, two-foot-long fangs in something like a grin. Jack took a hesitant step backward, trying to force a smile.

"Hello," he said weakly.

Lourdvang inclined his head, a sign of respect among dragons.

"Welcome, Jack. Any help is appreciated. The war turns against us."

"Dree!" a shrill voice shouted out.

Abi came running out of the tunnels, followed closely by her mother. Even in the caves Abi still looked far more composed than Dree ever was: Her hair was neatly braided and tied with a ribbon, though there was just a bit of dirt visible on her usually scrubbed cheeks. Dree's two little brothers were grabbing on to her mother's legs as they jogged over. Marny and Otto looked just as wild and carefree as ever. Both had light brown hair, always overgrown and unruly, and were laughing gaily as they ran. Dree felt her spirits lighten at the sight of them.

She picked up Abi into a firm hug, squeezing her until she laughed and shouted to be let down. Then their mom wrapped her in an equally firm embrace, and Dree let herself relax, feeling like a kid again for a second. She knelt down and mussed up her younger brothers' hair.

And then Rochin stepped up behind them, and her smile disappeared.

"What are you doing here?" Dree said coldly.

Erdath appeared as well, watching the encounter with his usual emotionless gaze.

"I . . . heard the family was in danger," Rochin said. "I wanted to help. I'm sorry about the last time I saw you . . . in the apartment when the drone attack came. I didn't mean to just run away like that. I was afraid. I didn't know what else to do."

"That's because you're a coward," Dree spat. "Always have been."

"Dree," her mother said.

Rochin held up a hand. "It's fine. I deserve that and more."

"We can worry about that later," Marcus said. "What's happening out there?" he asked, turning to Erdath and Lourdvang.

The two dragons exchanged a grave look. "It's not good," Lourdvang said, exhaustion apparent in his voice. "The drone attacks have become more frequent in the last week. Both on the humans and my kin. The Outliers are nearly extinct. The great factory churns out more and more drones every day. They fill the skies now."

"Did you get the Egg?" Erdath asked.

"Yes," Dree said. "But it's useless to us until we create another hybrid. We need time. And materials."

"We have retrieved another fallen drone," Lourdvang said. "But we need to do something in the meantime to stem the flow of drones. Too many humans and dragons are dying out there. The Resistance has made a plan to destroy the factory. To cut off Francis at the source and make sure he can't create any more drones."

Dree frowned. "The Resistance? What Resistance?"

Lourdvang looked at her for a moment, and then gestured with his head toward an adjoining cave—the same one where Marcus and Dree had built Baby Hybrid. Dree and Marcus started for the cavern, with Jack trailing close behind. He was still staring at the dragons in awe.

They reached the adjoining cavern, and Dree stopped in her tracks. There were about twenty men and women gathered in a circle, listening to someone speak. Charts and blueprints of the factory covered the walls. And in the middle of it all stood a man.

Dree stared at him in disbelief.

"Dad?"

Chapter 9

D ree stood in shock as her father rushed across the chamber, the others parting before him in near deference. Though Abelard's back was still a little bent, he stood straighter than Dree had seen him since she was a child. For a moment, she saw a Dragon Rider striding across the room toward her, tall and proud and stern. It seemed almost surreal, like she had slipped into a dream. And then it was her father again, and he pulled her into a fierce hug, his strong arms wrapped around her.

Dree buried her head into his shoulders. She felt her eyes stinging with unexpected tears. It was like her father had returned from the dead, and now he could protect her.

She pulled away, looking at him in amazement. "But how? What is this? When did . . . who are these people?"

Abelard ran a thumb along her cheek, smiling as he wiped away a tear. His face was covered in heavy stubble that crept down his neck, while his chestnut hair was unruly and spotted with flecks of dried mud. "This is the Resistance, Dree," he said. "Welcome."

He turned to Marcus and clasped his hand.

"Good to see you again, son."

"You too, sir," Marcus replied, exchanging a surprised look with Dree. "You look . . . different."

Abelard laughed, but a sudden hardness returned to his eyes. "Yes, I can imagine. A lot has happened since you were gone, even in so short a time. And yes . . . to me as well. But when the time came to stand up again, I think I realized that much of my broken body was here." He tapped his temple.

"I had quit, Dree. And I'm sorry for that. Francis tried to beat me . . . but he didn't finish the job. Perhaps I can finally hit back." He gestured toward a huddled group. "Let me introduce you both to some people."

He led them toward the group—about twenty strong— and a young man stepped forward. He had curly blond hair and bright blue eyes—he couldn't have been older than fourteen. He was tall, though, with the broad, strong shoulders of a fighter. He shook Dree's hand, squeezing hard.

He looked vaguely familiar, though she couldn't place him.

"This is Nathaniel Terrowin," Abelard said. "His mother was a great Rider, Allewyn Terrowin. Allewyn was in the Ruling Council when I was a Rider—she rode a wise old Sage named Olway. She passed away in the many years since, but her son is her spitting image. Nathaniel handles most of the missions into the city these days. He has been providing us with a lot of our intelligence."

"I've heard a lot about you two," Nathaniel said coolly. "Did you succeed on your mission?"

Dree bristled a little at the imperious tone in his voice. It reminded her of Master Wilhelm, her former employer, who treated her like she was dirt on his boots.

"Yes," Dree said, meeting his cool gaze, before turning back to her father "And who are the rest of the Resistance fighters?"

Abelard led them around the cavern, shaking hands and greeting the rest of the Resistance. There was a vast range of ages and occupations—teenagers to elders, butchers to tailors to former soldiers. But the one defining factor was that this group represented the last of the Dragon Riders and their families—twelve of the twenty-one in all. Some were actually former Riders that had been disbanded by Francis Xidorne, while others were the children of those now dead. They met Ciaran Rose, the daughter of famed Rider Helene Rose, who had died in battle some fifteen years ago. Though strikingly beautiful with her dark eyes and long, raven hair, Ciaran seemed quiet and reserved, giving Dree a curt nod and shaking her hand. But Dree saw a familiar fire in her eyes when they talked about the drones—Ciaran was bursting with rage. Dree liked her already. She noticed Marcus flushing bright red when he shook her hand, so she assumed he did too.

Dree and Marcus also met Eria Halton, another surviving Rider, who was even older than Dree's father. Eria had been famous in her day, riding on a temperamental Outlier called Norax. Now she was graying and wrinkled, her shoulders bent, but her dark eyes were big and intelligent and lively. Norax had been slaughtered by dragon hunters after Francis's revolution a decade earlier, and Eria was still thirsty for revenge. She shook Dree's hand, smiling. Eria had an iron grip.

"I have heard a lot about Abelard's daughter," she said, eyeing Dree's hands, as if looking for something there.

Dree wondered how much Eria knew about her . . . abilities, and if she was the one Abelard had been speaking to about Furies all those years ago. She did the same thing to Marcus, looking at his hands and into his eyes, and Marcus seemed uncomfortable under her intense gaze.

When they had met everyone, Dree and Marcus stepped aside with Abelard.

"Impressive," Marcus said. "This all started in the last week?"

Abelard nodded. "More or less. There was a Resistance movement all along in the city—underground, of course, mostly led by Eria, Ciaran, and Nathaniel here. But when the attacks continued on the city and no real progress was being made, they came to me to ask me to resume my leadership of the Resistance. I turned them down before, but even I couldn't just ignore the devastation any longer. I . . . reluctantly agreed."

"Reluctantly?" Dree asked.

"I was not sure I was the man for the job," he said. "I'm still not. But we will find out."

Dree smiled. "I think you're the perfect man for the job."

Nathaniel stepped up beside Abelard, forcing a smile. "I think we should get back to the planning," he said, annoyance tinging his voice. "We need to wipe out that drone factory as soon as possible." He eyed Dree. "Perhaps we can continue the reunion later."

"Yes," Abelard said, "you're right. Let's—"

He was cut off by the flapping of wings, and they turned to see two dragons settle to the ground beside them—one as golden as the morning sun, and the other a fiery, pinkish red, like the light of dusk.

Dree broke into a grin and rushed forward to give the golden dragon a hug. "Nolong!"

He knelt down and nuzzled her, looking pleased. Marcus turned to Vero, the red dragon.

"You've joined the Resistance?" he asked, surprised. "We were worried about you."

Vero inclined her head. "Rightly so. Helvath was not pleased that I assisted you in finding the Egg. He spared me death, but he exiled me from the Teeth. I admit, I did not really argue. It gave me a chance to find Nolong." She turned and looked at the golden dragon, her dark eyes flashing with adoration. "It had been too long."

Nolong met her eyes. "Yes. But of course there is no peace of mind yet. The drones have become more active than ever—many of my kind have been killed. We need to turn the tide of this war . . . and soon."

"We can help with that," Dree said, finally slipping off her pack. She opened it and pulled out the Egg. Its red and orange flames rippled down the smooth ebony surface and over her entire arm.

"The Egg," Vero whispered. "You found it."

"Yeah," Dree said. "And we need to figure out how to use it to—"

She stopped as an explosion suddenly roared through the air, shaking the entire cavern and nearly causing her to drop the Egg. A second explosion echoed through the caves, and shattered rock started to rain down from the ceiling, causing the group to scramble and cover their heads for protection.

"What is that?" Dree asked.

Abelard looked toward the cave entrance.

"We're under attack."

Chapter 10

Flaking rock and stalactites continued to rain down from the ceiling as everyone scrambled toward the main cavern.

"Get into the tunnels!" Abelard shouted. "Get everyone down there now!"

Dree and Marcus stuck close together, sheltering their heads from the falling debris. A huge boulder nearly twice his size crashed into the ground beside Marcus, and he quickly jumped out of the way as it shattered and sent shards of rock flying in all directions.

They heard an agonizing roar as a rock landed on Vero's back, leaving a large wound as it bounced off, and she gnashed her teeth and prepared to launch herself toward the main cavern entrance, where a line of grim Nightwings were standing guard.

Nolong stepped in front of her. "No," he said firmly. "They are waiting for us to attack. They will gun you down swiftly." He turned and looked at Marcus. "Get everyone deeper into the tunnels. Hurry!"

Many of the humans and dragons were already headed deeper into the cavern, but Dree turned to help corral Abi and the boys, while Marcus looked around to see if there were any other stragglers. Another explosion rocked the cave, causing him to stumble to the ground.

Marcus noticed a mother struggling with her two young children. He jumped to his feet to scoop up one of the little boys. He turned to the mother, saying, "Let's go."

She grabbed the girl and they hurried across the cavern, almost falling several times under the barrage. A stalactite slammed into the ground ahead of them, splintering with an earsplitting crack.

Marcus looked around and saw dragons and humans being hit by the falling rock. One dragon was pinned in the corner, while an older man was lying on the ground nearby, unconscious or worse. Everyone was screaming and running.

They reached the back tunnels, where Erdath ushered everyone deeper into the mountain. The caverns and tunnels ran many miles beneath the surface, and it would be far safer there. It would probably have been safer to stay down there all the time, but it was cool and dark in the depths, and most of the humans preferred to be near the fresh air. He suspected that wasn't an option anymore.

Marcus put down the young boy. "Run with your mother now," he said.

"Thank you," the mother replied, and they hurried down the tunnel.

"Where are you going?" Erdath called as Marcus took off into the main cavern again.

"To help!" Marcus shouted back, rushing toward the unconscious man.

Lourdvang, Dree, and Abelard were also in the main cavern, dodging the falling rocks as they tried to get the scattered humans and dragons to safety. Lourdvang grabbed the boulder pinning one dragon by his tail and threw it off, allowing the frail elder Nightwing to head for the tunnels. Marcus knelt next to the unconscious man, grimacing at the caked blood on his white hair where a falling rock had hit him. As Marcus struggled to get under the man's arm and pick him up, Dree appeared beside him, taking the other arm.

"Hurry," she said tensely.

They half walked, half dragged the man across the cavern as the whole mountain continued shaking under the constant barrage. Marcus glanced back at the opening, where at least twenty dragons were now lined up shoulder to shoulder, defending the entrance against any incursion. But the drones clearly weren't entering the cavern yet. Nolong was right—they were trying to draw the dragons out into open air.

They made it to the back tunnel, and Nathaniel and another Resistance fighter rushed forward to take the man who Dree and Marcus were helping. Nathaniel looked at Dree and Marcus.

"You should get below," he ordered. "It's too dangerous up here for kids."

"We're fine," Dree snapped, glaring back at him as they rushed back into the main cavern.

"What is he . . . like fourteen?" Marcus asked.

"I know," Dree said. She saw Abelard helping another fallen woman and ran to help.

Marcus paused, eyeing the open entrance. He knew that if the drones decided to enter the cavern and breached the line of defending dragons, they could seal off all the tunnels and destroy the Resistance's supplies. Food, water, and heaps of armor and weaponry were all stashed in the main cavern here. If that was destroyed, the Resistance would be helpless—even if they managed to escape the destroyed tunnels. He looked around the chamber at the piles of fallen stone.

"Lourdvang," he shouted. "Help me!"

Marcus grabbed some of the fallen rock and ran toward the entrance, trying to show Lourdvang what he wanted to do. The huge Nightwing understood immediately. He began grabbing the fallen boulders and stalactites and piling them by the entrance to create a barricade. The dragon guards quickly caught on, and soon all of the fallen stone was being used to block the entrance. When they ran short of the existing rubble, the Nightwings ripped stone from the cracking walls themselves, caving in the entrance with their incredible strength. A massive defensive wall began to form, blocking most of the opening from attack. There was still a gap, but at least it would give them something to hide behind.

They were just in time.

Baby Hybrid dropped into view outside, flanked by two Trackers. Marcus felt his heart sink at the sight of her. He remembered lovingly creating the hybrid with Dree, and their pride when it had flown out of this very mountain. And he remembered the feeling of watching it crash into the palace, left in the hands of Francis. A part of him had hoped that she would be too damaged to be used again, but he had known better. They had built her too well. She still looked the same—fiery red eyes glowing in her expertly welded head, machine guns and missiles sitting below her two great metal wings. He almost wanted to run out and try to take her back.

And then Baby Hybrid opened fire with her machine guns, sending a deadly flurry of bullets into the cavern. Marcus dove behind the wall of stone and saw Dree and Abelard slam into the ground behind him.

One of the Nightwings wasn't so lucky. The bullets chewed into his wings and riddled his chest, and the beautiful black dragon hit the ground, the life leaving his eyes. Lourdvang ducked down beside Marcus and let out a terrible roar, enraged at the death of a fellow Nightwing. The rest of the dragons followed suit, creating a horrendous din in the cavern. Several burst around the partially finished barricade, unleashing a wave of fire, but they too were gunned down by Baby Hybrid and the drones. One at least made it far enough to spew fire onto the three drones, and they quickly scattered out of the way.

Erdath rushed forward, blowing a massive smoke screen over the opening, obscuring the sky.

"Gather the dead!" he shouted. "Finish the barricade!"

The dragons quickly pulled back the bodies, while others collapsed the ceiling. Marcus and the other humans pulled back, until a massive pile of stone blocked almost the whole opening, letting just a few streams of light in through the top. The smoke began to clear, revealing the dead dragons—five of them, their lifeless bodies lying in the dust and haze. It looked like a half-formed nightmare—too foggy to make out at any real details.

"It's the fourth attack this week," Abelard said. "Though they haven't tried to take the entrance yet. They've just been pulverizing the mountain. I fear next time they will come for the kill."

He turned to Marcus and Dree.

"The plan isn't completely ready yet, but we can't waste any more time. We attack the factory tonight."

Abelard and Erdath stood in front of a large group of humans and dragons, deep in Forost in a lower cavern they called the war room. Many of the humans wore black, fire-resistant armor and bore spears and swords, while the massive dragons stood grimly behind them. Marcus and Dree stayed toward the back with Jack and the rest of Dree's family. Jack had a gash on his head following the attack, but otherwise he was unhurt. He had been quizzing Marcus and Dree furiously on their creation of Baby Hybrid and its capabilities. Jack was looking for any way to help, and he wanted to take the lead in building a second version. Marcus knew the guilt was weighing very heavily on him.

"We lost five more of our kin today," Erdath said gravely, smoke billowing from his nostrils. "They died defending Forost and the Resistance from our enemies. Koro, Levithan, Devat, Mara, and Jerwyn—may they fly forever in the light of the sun. Let us remember them."

The dragons inclined their heads, growling low in their throats. The humans followed suit.

"The time has come to strike back," Abelard broke in, stepping beside Erdath and looking out at the gathered warriors. "The drones continue to pour forth from the factory in ever greater numbers. We cannot fight an enemy who has infinite reinforcements. And so tonight we attack the factory, and we destroy it. At least then we'll know exactly how many drones we have to defeat."

There was a murmur of agreement around the room. Abelard turned to a drawing propped up on a wooden stand beside him. They were schematics of the factory—Dree's mother had once worked inside.

"It will be dangerous," Abelard continued. "We will first attack with a stealth force of human fighters to help neutralize the human guards and air defenses. There will be many people working in the factory, so we must make sure to evacuate. And if we don't take out the air defenses, the skies will be too dangerous for dragons. Once the factory is cleared, we will send up the red flare. Only then will the dragons swoop in to burn the factory to the ground."

"We should just leave the people in there," Nathaniel snarled from the front.

"We are not murderers," Erdath countered solemnly. "We are better than our enemies."

Abelard nodded. "We need volunteers to stay here and work on building more of the fire-resistant armor. As you know, none of us can ride the dragons without it. We'll need as many suits as possible for our next battle with the drones. Every Rider will need a suit, and right now we only have a handful."

"Marcus and Dree can ride without the armor," Lourdvang said.

The entire group of Resistance fighters turned to them, and Marcus shifted uncomfortably.

"You can touch the dragons?" Ciaran asked, looking at them in amazement. "Both of you?"

Dree hesitated, and then laid her bare hand on Lourdvang's leg. Marcus did the same.

"Furies," Eria said loudly. "I knew it. The first in two generations."

There was a lot of muttering and incredulous looks in the chamber, and Marcus could see Nathaniel staring at them, looking even less friendly than before. Dree's mother was staring with equal surprise, while Rochin and Abi were both wide-eyed. Rochin even took a little step back, as if afraid of his little sister.

"Why does Nathaniel look like he wants to punch us?" Marcus whispered.

Dree shook her head. "I don't know. Like I said, I don't think Furies are very common."

"Have there ever been two at once?" Ciaran asked, looking to Eria.

Eria stepped forward, eyeing Marcus and Dree. "No. Not that I know of."

"What does it . . . mean to be a Fury?" Dree's mother asked. "Is she . . . is she going to be like the last one . . . ?"

Dree looked at her mom, frowning. "What last one?"

Eria turned to Dree. "Not all know the tale . . . we did much to hide it. Marcus, you should perhaps know a bit more about what you are. A Fury is the rarest of Dragon Riders. A Dragon Rider is such because they have descended from the ancient order and share a natural bond with a certain dragon. They are proficient at riding and weaponry, and they are supposed to maintain the highest level of honor. A Fury is the same—but they are also fire incarnate. Dragon fire moves in their body, and they have an unusual ability to wield it, and to be impervious to it as an attack. Even the fire of Helvath would pass them over without harm. Weaponry and illness can still kill them, but never fire. Furies are the greatest Riders . . . and the most dangerous."

"Dangerous?" Marcus asked.

Eria nodded. "The last Fury was a man named Dareon. He almost destroyed the Riders, and killed many of our grandparents. They finally exiled him from Dracone, at great cost to the Riders and Dracone."

Marcus and Dree exchanged a concerned look.

"But we each forge our own paths," Eria said. "And you two must find your own."

Lourdvang cut in. "For now those two can just scout the factory and stay back from the battle."

"We're going in on the ground," Dree said sharply, turning to him and narrowing her eyes.

Lourdvang scowled and blew out a puff of smoke.

"I'll stay and work on the armor," Rochin said loudly, raising his hand

Dree snorted. "You just want to avoid the front lines, big brother."

"Dree," Marcus said. "Give him a break. Your father asked for volunteers."

She crossed her arms and turned back to the front, scowling.

"Good," Abelard said, nodding at his son. "I will assign a few more to help you, Rochin. It is indeed an important responsibility. Nathaniel, get your team together. Dree and Marcus, you're with me."

Erdath nodded. "I will lead the dragon attack from the air. We will be waiting for the signal."

The room suddenly broke into a hundred conversations, and Marcus turned to Dree.

"That was . . . different," he said. "Why didn't you tell me about Dareon?"

"I didn't know about him either. I guess my dad wanted to keep that part from me."

Marcus fidgeted. "Do you think that's like a . . . Fury thing to do? Turn evil?"

"I'm sure it was just him. I don't know. I'll talk to my dad."

Suddenly, Abi stepped in and interrupted their conversation. "Can I go on the mission with you guys?" she asked, her voice small but eager.

Dree smiled and knelt down beside her little sister. "It's too dangerous for you out there, little one. You stay here with the others. Maybe you can work on the armor? And keep an eye on Rochin for me," she muttered, eyeing her brother darkly.

Abi drooped her head in disappointment. "I will. Will you be safe out there?"

Dree lifted her sister's chin and looked her in the eye. "Always. Now I have to go talk to Dad. You be good, all right?"

As Dree spoke to her little sister, Jack took Marcus aside.

"I checked out what we have for hybrid supplies. There are some parts from a damaged drone they captured, but it's not enough. I'll stay here and start working on a new hybrid, but I need more material: a new computer core, some weapons systems, extra wiring. I need to create an energy transferal for the Egg."

Marcus nodded. "I'll see what I can find at the factory. I'll bring back whatever I can."

Jack put his hand on Marcus's shoulder, meeting his eyes. "I'm proud of you, Marcus. And so is your father."

Marcus forced a smile. "Do you think he's okay?"

"I do," Jack said. "He knows too much for anyone to hurt him. He'll be there waiting when we get back—trust me. And then we'll get him out. For now, go stop those drones. And be careful, understand?"

Marcus nodded and then followed Dree to the other side of the war room, where they saw Nathaniel talking to a young Sage. The golden dragon was about the size of an elephant, and his scales were still a bit pale and dull— apparently, the gold grew more magnificent with age. He was talking quietly with Nathaniel, and Marcus nudged Dree and walked a bit closer to hear.

"It's too dangerous," Nathaniel said.

The dragon growled. "I want to help. I need to help. My mother—"

"I know," Nathaniel said softly. "I'm sorry, Emmett. But you're still so young."

"So are you," Emmett replied sullenly. "Please let me join. I need to do *something*."

Nathaniel looked at him for a long moment, as if considering the young dragon, and then sighed. "Fine. But you stay well back until the signal, understand? And stick close to Erdath at all times."

The dragon broke into a toothy grin. "My first mission."

Nathaniel laughed grimly. "But not your last, I'm afraid."

Marcus and Dree exchanged a look and continued on toward Abelard.

"Maybe Nathaniel's not a total loss," Dree muttered.

Marcus laughed. "Maybe."

Abelard turned to them, a long sword hanging in a sheath at his side. He looked like a warrior.

"Ready?" he asked them grimly.

Marcus and Dree nodded.

"Good," he said. "Let's gather the troops. It's time to hit back."

Chapter 11

Dree stood crouched in the tall grass at the base of a mountain, surrounded by Resistance fighters. There were fourteen of them gathered for the attack, including Dree and Marcus, while the remainder had stayed behind to help guard Forost.

Marcus stood next to her, and both kept their eyes fixed on the massive factory that stood on the edge of Dracone. Once a steel mill, the building rose up like a mountain itself, its fortress-like walls rising as tall as the highest of the palace towers. A few white lights glared on the outside—the only building in Dracone to have them. They shone like stars. The whole facility seemed like a strange blot on the quiet, darkened city landscape.

The factory was also surrounded by guards. Dree could make out at least twenty of them in the darkness, all standing with long spears slung over their shoulders. They were members of the Protectorate. It was odd to see speared warriors defending a factory that churned out technology as advanced as drones, but George told Marcus he had never introduced handheld guns, and it seemed Francis thankfully had no idea how to build them, judging by the fact that none of the Protectorate had any. But they were manning large crossbows, trebuchets, and other aerial defenses to guard against dragon attacks. The Resistance would have to take those down first.

"The guard shift change takes place in the next few minutes," Abelard said to the group, his low, deep voice carrying over the still nighttime air. "As soon as this shift leaves, we make our move. Remember, the priority is to knock out any air defenses and get all of the factory workers to safety. We won't have long before the drones respond from wherever Xidorne is keeping them. When we get the last worker out, we give the signal and the dragons will attack."

Dree looked back, where she knew at least twenty dragons were perched on the mountainside like enormous birds of prey, waiting to make their move. Lourdvang was among them, as were Erdath and the young Sage, Emmett.

"Marcus and Dree need to collect extra drone pieces to help with the construction of the new hybrid," Abelard continued. "So make sure you are ready to help them get the materials out. Other than that, good luck."

Everyone turned back to the factory, and within minutes the guards began to head for the front gate, where more armed men were waiting to take over the next shift. All moved with military precision.

"Go!" Abelard commanded.

The Resistance fighters broke into a swift jog through the meadow, moving in a pack. It was a cool night, and Dree felt the breeze washing over her as they hurried toward the chain-link fence that had been built around the factory. It stood at least ten feet tall, but it was vulnerable. She and a few others stepped forward with metal cutters, and they quickly snipped openings in the fence. The Resistance fighters streamed in like rainwater through a leaky roof, spreading out and breaking into a full run as they approached the factory. A group of fighters broke off to go dismantle a massive crossbow standing outside the wall—it was armed with gleaming iron arrows designed to tear through dragon wings.

The rest of the group headed for the factory, with Dree in the lead. She nodded to Marcus as they sidled toward a side door. The night was still quiet, and the rest of the fighters reached the wall in safety.

"Go," Abelard said, and Nathaniel opened the door and hurried inside, clutching a sword.

There was a clash of steel, and when Dree came in she saw a guard lying on the floor, unmoving. Nathaniel cleaned his sword, his young, handsome face set like a stone.

"Come on," he barked. "Find the workers!"

Dree and Marcus rounded the corner, but both stopped in disbelief. The drone factory was no longer just hidden beneath the floor. The entire mill had been retrofitted now, and an assembly line of drones filled the massive space. Workers were welding wings to hulls, overseeing massive forges, and monitoring machines that George had created to fabricate computer cores and wiring and missiles. The entire factory looked like a living, breathing organism— churning out nothing but death. Half-finished drones waited everywhere: Destroyers, Trackers, Surveyors. There must have been fifty drones under construction. A brand-new army.

Marcus ran to a huge bank of controls nearby, scanning over the screens. He found a red lever at the side and pulled it down. Immediately, the machinery stopped and the conveyor belts ground to a halt.

The factory workers all looked up, confused, and Abelard's voice rang out.

"All of you . . . get out now! This building is going to be destroyed." He gestured to his fighters. "Get them out!"

Nathaniel and the others rushed forward, ushering the bewildered men and women toward the door. The fighters weren't overly gentle. Dree saw Nathaniel shove one older man toward the door, causing him to lose his balance and hit the ground hard, groaning. Dree stepped in front of Nathaniel, glaring at him.

"Stop that!" she snarled.

"He's building those things, and you are going to protect him?" Nathaniel asked. "As far as I'm concerned, he deserves to be left here."

The old man struggled back to his feet, grimacing. "We were ordered by the Prime Minister to work here," he said nervously. "We didn't choose it."

"You could have shut it down," Nathaniel said sharply.

"They would have killed us," he said. "The Protectorate have been watching us like hawks."

Dree stared daggers at Nathaniel and then helped the man toward the door. Soon the workers were flooding out, and she looked around the factory, searching for Marcus. She spotted him inspecting parts next to the assembly line. Marcus and Jack had told Dree what to look for, so she hurried over to another supply area. She found what looked like computer cores and threw one in her bag—a big bulky cylinder that must have weighed twenty pounds at least. She turned to grab some extra wiring when an alarm suddenly went off, sounding like an old war siren. Black armored guards rushed in from the front entrance, carrying swords and spears.

It was time to go.

"Marcus!" Dree called, turning for the exit. "We need to get out of here!"

He nodded, but continued scooping up materials. Abelard was already starting for the exit with the other fighters, and Nathaniel was ushering out the last of the workers.

"Marcus!" Nathaniel called. "Now!"

Dree was halfway to the exit when Marcus finally turned and started running. He didn't make it. A guard burst out from behind a partition and body-checked him hard, slamming into one of the conveyor belts. Marcus kept his footing, but he grabbed his ribs, wincing, and the towering guard punched him across the face with a gloved right fist, knocking him onto the ground. Dree screamed and turned to help.

"I'll get him," Nathaniel shouted, racing ahead of her.

But he wasn't needed. Marcus looked up from the floor, holding his jaw. Blood spilled out between his fingers. Dree saw immediately that something wasn't right. His eyes looked . . . orange.

Marcus clenched his fists and turned sharply, rising at the same time. Fire swarmed over his fist and arm as he turned, and he stuck his hand out and hit the guard with a fireball, sending him flying backward. The man hit the wall and crashed into the ground, unconscious, as Marcus stood seething, the fire flickering out around him. Dree watched in fascination. She saw the danger too late.

The fire was streaming over some of the power cells, and one of them was beginning to overheat.

"Marcus!" she shouted.

Nathaniel got there first. He tackled Marcus, and both boys went tumbling under the conveyor belt just as an explosion rocketed through the air. Nathaniel and Marcus emerged from the other side of the conveyor, having only just escaped the explosion. Marcus's eyes and hands were normal again, and he and Nathaniel ran toward the exit.

Dree joined them. "Marcus, what was that—"

"I don't know," he said, shooting Dree an unsure glance before continuing on.

They ran out through the exit and across the supply yard toward the fence. The factory workers and Resistance fighters were streaming through, and when Abelard saw them, he took out a flare and lit it.

An explosion of red streamed up into the sky, hanging there like a supernova. The signal was given. In the distance, massive black shapes began to swoop off the mountain, silhouettes against the moonlight.

"Faster!" Abelard hollered.

The last of the workers made it through the fence and sprinted across the field in a panicked mob, while Abelard waved Dree, Marcus, and Nathaniel through. He followed them just as the Protectorate guards burst through the factory doors, charging after the Resistance. They couldn't catch up in time, though.

The first dragons swooped in, and the night became awash with fire. As Dree ran into the meadow, she saw flames consuming the factory, now burning like a torch. Dragons circled overhead, diving down to attack. She knew Lourdvang was there, unleashing his fury.

Within minutes, the structure was collapsing in on itself, and the group had moved farther into the field toward the mountains. The factory workers had been released, and they all fled back into the city. As the Resistance made their way into the mountains, they stopped in the valley and looked back. The attack was over, and the factory was destroyed. The mission had been a success.

"Victory!" Nathaniel shouted, pumping his fist.

The cry was repeated, echoing through the night.

Dree hugged her father, and he beamed.

"This was the first step," he said. "Now we have a finite number of drones to fight. The tide is finally turning."

Dree smiled. "I'm proud of you, Dad."

Abelard smiled back, and they turned toward the mountains.

But the celebration didn't last long. The dragons swooped down around them, their mood sullen. Lourdvang and Erdath held an injured dragon between them, and as they lowered him to the ground, the small dragon cried out. A massive steel arrow stuck out of his golden torso.

Nathaniel rushed forward. "Emmett!"

Dree recognized the young dragon who had begged Nathaniel to join the fight. She looked at the arrow in his side and felt sick.

If they didn't move quickly, Emmett was going to die.

Chapter 12

Emmett let out a deep, rasping groan, and Marcus and Dree rushed forward to help. Lourdvang grabbed the barbed iron arrow with his teeth and yanked it cleanly out of the young dragon's side, eliciting a spurt of black blood and a terrible howl from Emmett. Nathaniel was shouting for help at no one in particular, and Marcus pulled off his jacket and pressed it tightly to the wound, stopping the flow of blood as best as he could.

"We need to get him back to Nolong," Erdath growled. "He may be able to heal the wound. A Sage's fire can mend most injuries . . . it's the young one's only chance."

"He won't make it," Marcus said, pressing with both hands. "We need to stop the bleeding."

Erdath put a giant clawed limb over the wound, holding the jacket firmly down, and Marcus stepped back. Emmett groaned in pain again, his black eyes barely staying open.

Nathaniel leaned in close. "You're going to be okay," he said, stroking Emmett's nose.

Abelard motioned to the rest of the Resistance fighters. "Keep moving. Get back to Forost." He turned to Erdath. "The drones will sweep the area soon. I'm sure they're already on their way."

Erdath nodded and turned to the dragons. "Lourdvang and I will take Emmett back. Inform Nolong to be ready when we get there. Keep the skies clear for the humans. Do not engage any drones."

Immediately, the dragons took to the skies, their enormous bodies and wings practically blocking out the moon.

Erdath turned back to Marcus. "We need to hurry."

He lifted his claw from Emmett's torso, and Marcus inspected the wound. Dree leaned in next to him.

"Can we bandage it?" she asked.

"We'll just have to keep pressure on it," Marcus responded. He leaned in close to Emmett, making sure to keep his voice calm and gentle. "Emmett, you'll need to keep your claw on the wound while Lourdvang and Erdath carry you. Do you think you can do that?"

Emmett grunted in response.

"You'll be fine," Nathaniel said again, still sounding frantic. "Think of your mother. This is nothing but a scratch."

Dree looked at Abelard questioningly, and Abe lowered his voice. "Emmett's mother was Erwing, Nathaniel's mother's dragon."

Dree nodded, and Marcus applied Abe's and her jackets to the wound before placing Emmett's claw hand against them. But when Lourdvang and Erdath went to pick him up, Emmett cried out in pain.

"I don't think he can make the trip," Marcus said. "He needs to rest. We need Nolong to get here. I'm sure he'll come looking for us. We have no choice but to wait."

Erdath looked to the sky, searching for drones overhead. There was worry in his eyes, but he nodded. "Okay," he said. "So we wait."

Dawn was not too far away. Red-and-orange light soon filled the sky, pushing the shadows away. Marcus, Dree, Abe, and Lourdvang sat together, while Nathaniel and Erdath kept watch for Nolong. Thankfully, Francis seemed more concerned with protecting the city from more attacks, and he hadn't sent the drones to find them . . . yet.

"It was a victory," Abe said, "but we have a long way to go."

"Still," Marcus agreed, "it was a start. Francis can't rebuild that factory himself."

"Can he get at your father?" Lourdvang asked.

Marcus shook his head. "My father is in CIA custody. He's safe for now."

At the mention of George, Marcus felt a surge of guilt over leaving his father behind. Maybe they should have gone back for him. Maybe they could have overpowered the CIA agent. Was he a bad son for running? Would he have been so quick to abandon a father who had raised him and been there his whole life? That thought just made him feel even guiltier. He wondered if he would ever be able to just forgive his father for leaving him. He would never know until they had a little time to mend their relationship. They had finally started, and then he had been torn away once again. Marcus promised himself that he would go rescue his father as soon as possible and then bring him back to Dracone where he belonged.

"So we are dealing with a finite number of drones," Dree said. "It's something, at least. Francis may stop his attacks on the villages and outskirts. It buys the people some more time."

"We may have been too late for that. Most of the villages are destroyed," Abe said quietly. "There are only a few left. Cardon, Maise, and Ura. Most of the survivors from the other villages had fled to the city or taken refuge in the mountains. Many have died. Francis has effectively cleared the way for his complete control."

"Except for the Resistance and the dragons," Marcus said.

"Exactly. If we keep fighting, then the war isn't over yet."

"Francis is going to be furious over losing the factory,"

Dree said. "He's going to send his full army against us."

Abe nodded. "Perhaps. But we will just have to be ready."

"We're going to need to get at Francis himself eventually," Marcus pointed out.

"He is well protected," Lourdvang cut in, turning his head back to the distant city. "Drones circling the palace at all times. Guards and antiaircraft weapons manning the castle. It won't be easy."

"But it is necessary," Abe said. "He has to pay for all of this death and destruction."

"Finally!" Erdath suddenly growled.

Marcus turned and caught a flash of gold and saw Nolong swooping low through the valley, heading right for them. He looked like a stray burst of sunlight. Marcus jumped to his feet, hoping desperately that Nolong could save Emmett. The young dragon was growing weaker.

"What happened?" Nolong asked gruffly, landing beside the group and heading straight for Emmett. "They just said he was injured."

"Iron barb in the side," Erdath said, following him. "Can you heal him?"

Nolong scanned over the young dragon and then focused on the wound. "Time will tell."

The group gathered around as Nolong began to blow a rippling, autumn-gold fire onto the wound. Emmett cried out, but Erdath held him down. Slowly the flames began to bind the wound.

Marcus watched in amazement. It was like a weld—sealing the golden scales back together. Finally, Nolong stepped away, and Emmett stopped struggling.

Nolong looked at the group. "He will live."

Nathaniel let out a relieved gasp, and Marcus and Dree both grinned. There had been enough death of late.

"Give him a few moments, and then we will carry him back," Erdath said.

Nathaniel ran his hand along Emmett's snout, comforting the young dragon.

Marcus watched them for a moment, thinking that Nathaniel was a lot different than he let on, and then looked back toward the city. He froze.

"Impossible," he whispered.

A solid line of drones was converging on the city from the south. They almost blocked the sun, there were so many. Marcus counted at least fifty. It was a wave of death, sweeping across the sky toward the ruined factory. It seemed that Francis was consolidating his forces around the city. If the Resistance attacked the city again, the drones would be waiting.

Abe and Dree stepped up beside him, both looking grim.

"Now the war really begins," Dree whispered.

Marcus turned to her. "And we are severely outnumbered."

Chapter 13

Marcus and Dree looked around Forost's decimated central cavern, pockmarked with bullet holes and jagged craters from the missiles. Baby Hybrid and the drones had attacked again during the assault on the factory and had destroyed much of the Resistance's food and water supply. Some of the fire-resistant metal had survived, as it had been dragged down into the tunnels earlier to be fitted and shaped for armor, but the rest had been blown apart. They no longer had enough metal to arm all of the would-be Dragon Riders.

"It seems we both decided to make a pre-emptive attack," Marcus said, shaking his head.

Dree scowled. "Our remaining supplies won't last us much longer. A week or two at most."

"We can get more," Marcus said.

"How?" Dree replied. "The drones are covering the sky. If we go back into Dracone, we'll be killed."

They were standing alone in the middle of the cavern while Abe and Erdath spoke in the far corner. Nolong had carried Emmett into a side cavern and was letting him rest—the Sage had managed to mend the worst of the injuries, and Emmett was going to survive. Nathaniel didn't move from his side.

Lourdvang walked up behind them. "No one was hurt," he said. "The guards retreated in time."

"That's something at least," Dree said. "We can't afford any more losses."

Lourdvang nodded. "We may already be too few."

Marcus looked over the pile of rubble, thinking about all the destruction that the drones had caused. He pictured the shattered outskirts of the city, and the smoking ruins of the outlying villages. So many lives had been lost because of his father and Jack's inventions. He wondered again if his father had known what these drones might be used for. If George had, even for a while, believed in Francis's vision.

If that was the case, Marcus didn't think he could ever forgive his father for all of this. If that was the case, then maybe George deserved to be in prison.

Marcus snapped back to attention when he saw Nathaniel emerge from a side cavern, his face ashen and grim.

"How is Emmett?" Dree asked immediately.

"He'll live," Nathaniel said. "Just barely made it. But Nolong says the damage to his wing muscles and nerves are beyond his skill to heal. Nolong doesn't think Emmett will ever fly again."

Lourdvang made a low noise, shaking his head in dismay. For a dragon to lose his ability to fly was a terrible thing—a greater curse than anything they could suffer. Dragons lived for the open air and the cold northern wind beneath their wings. They all knew that young Emmett would be devastated.

Dree put her hand on Nathaniel's shoulder. "At least he's alive. You should take some comfort in that."

Nathaniel nodded, but his expression remained stern. "Excuse me. I need to go talk to Abe."

He stalked off, and Marcus and Dree headed into the tunnels to see Jack, whom they found bent over a disorganized tangle of scrap metal and circuitry, connecting the interior workings of Teen Hybrid, as Jack had started calling it after learning about the moniker for the first version. He said it definitely would be more advanced than the first one, but that he had no idea how it was really supposed to work or how it would turn out when he was finished, so "teen" felt suitable. Marcus and Dree had just laughed and taken on the name. Teen Hybrid's skeleton was slowly starting to form, though it was in the early stages. Jack looked up and grinned.

"Marcus! You're all right."

"I am," Marcus said. "How's it going here?"

Jack sighed. "There's still a long way to go, I'm afraid. Were you able to find more parts?"

Marcus nodded, and he and Dree presented Jack with what they had been able to collect: two computer cores, multiple power cells, and a lot more circuitry. Jack looked at the haul and nodded. "That will help. But I could also use a welder," he said, glancing at Dree.

Dree grinned. "I'll get my stuff. Marcus and Lourdvang will help too. We need to move fast."

Dree hurried off to get her welding equipment with Lourdvang close behind.

Marcus watched them go, and then turned to Jack. "Can I ask you something?"

"Of course."

"Why did you and my father create the drones? I know there are drones back on Earth, but they're not nearly this sophisticated. Giving them artificial intelligence . . . it's made them far more dangerous. I just . . . Why were you working on this project?"

Jack looked at him for a moment and then laid down the circuitry he was holding.

"I was working on it because your father asked me to."

Marcus frowned. "So it was his idea."

"Yes," Jack admitted. "We had become friends after he read my work on artificial intelligence. I had worked for the CIA before, but I wasn't working on anything specific at the time—just general AI research. He told me he had a new project, and he needed my help."

Jack looked down at the cannibalized drone.

"I'll admit, I was hesitant. I didn't want to contribute to any kind of war, and when George told me how heavily armed these drones would be, I objected. I asked him if he really wanted to use these against his fellow man. He said no. He said they were to serve as protection against any other enemies, ones far more dangerous than I could ever know. I was skeptical of the project, but he was my friend, and I trusted him." Jack sighed and ran his hands through his hair. "Your father is a brilliant man. So, despite my misgivings, we started the project. And when we had the designs and were about to get them approved for final construction, he came to me and told me he had to go. By then he had told me about the portal, about his past. I even knew about the dragons. I told him to stay with you, but he wouldn't. He said he had no choice, so he left you with me and disappeared."

Marcus walked along the drone hulk, softly touching its massive machines guns and missile launchers.

"So he really did want to use the drones to destroy the dragons. That was always the plan."

"I believe so," Jack said. "But he was seeking revenge; he wasn't thinking straight."

Marcus turned away, clenching his fists. "My father is a murderer, Jack. He created all of this turmoil."

"No," Jack said. "He made a terrible mistake by setting this in motion, but this Francis guy—he's the one who took it to the next level. Your father never would have set out to harm so many, I'm sure of it. Of course, if I had known what it was being used for . . ."

Marcus heard the regret in his voice and thought of something.

"You must be angry with him. He used you for the AI and then stole the design from you."

Jack nodded. "That occurred to me too. But a man seeking vengeance will do foolish things. It doesn't always mean he's a bad person. But it does mean that he has to try to find redemption."

The silence held for a while, and then Marcus just sighed and picked up a computer core. "I wonder what it's like to have a normal family."

Jack snorted. "Boring. Trust me. But enough reflection. Let's get to work."

"Marcus!" Dree shouted from the door.

Marcus turned to her and immediately knew something was wrong. She looked furious. "What's wrong?" he asked.

"My father is gathering the Resistance fighters," she said. "They want to strike the palace tonight."

When Marcus and Dree arrived in the war room, Abelard and Nathaniel were already surrounded by Resistance fighters and dragons waiting to receive their orders. Abelard paced back and forth at the front of the room, his tired face flushed and angry.

"We cannot wait any longer," he said gruffly. "Today another village was destroyed. One of our scouts saw the remains of Cardon from the air today. It was once a beautiful town . . . I remember sailing above it, watching them plow the wheat fields. Now it is just a smoking crater."

There were angry murmurs around the room. Abelard continued. "Too many lives are being lost. The drones continue to attack the defenseless. I know we are not as prepared as we hoped, but the time is now. Francis will be reeling from our successful attack on the factory. We disrupted his plans, and he will be trying to reallocate his remaining drones. For a while, he may be too busy to plan a proper defense. We must strike."

A roar of approval went up from the fighters and dragons, creating a noise so thunderous it shook the walls.

Nathaniel walked next to Abelard, scowling. He addressed the crowd. "We break into the palace tonight and kill Francis. With him gone, we can take control of the drones and ground them all. Forever. Who's ready to fight?"

Another roar went up. Marcus started to step forward to say something, but Dree beat him to it.

"No," she said firmly, her voice carrying across the room.

Everyone turned to her.

"What?" Nathaniel said, narrowing his eyes.

Dree walked to the front of the room, and Marcus and Lourdvang exchanged a knowing look.

Someone was about to get a lecture.

"We are not ready," she said angrily. "We need Teen Hybrid and the Egg. We went all the way to Earth to find it, and now you want to attack without our two greatest weapons? Did you see how many drones there were? If we go in without Teen Hybrid, we're all dead. The Resistance is over."

"We're not afraid," Nathaniel snarled.

"Well, you should be," Dree snapped. "We only get one shot to take back Dracone. If you go in now and lose to Francis, the Resistance is over. All of this fighting and planning will have been for nothing."

Nathaniel turned to Abelard. "If we wait, we could miss our window to attack. We have to move now."

Abelard looked between them, and then his gray eyes hardened. "I'm sorry, Dree. We attack."

"It's a mistake," Dree said, feeling her temper rising. "If we lose, we throw away everything."

"What do you know about strategy?" Nathaniel scoffed.

"I know that you wait until you are ready," she replied coolly.

Abelard sighed and turned away. "We have to be ready now. I'm sorry."

Dree slumped, defeated.

"Just a minute now," a new voice cut in.

They turned to see Dree's mother pushing through the crowd. She was staring at Abelard like he had just spilled something on the carpet back at home. "Your daughter is the only one here who has successfully taken on those drones," she snapped, looking around the war room. "Dree and Marcus are the only reason any of us are still alive, in case you have forgotten. They got us to safety when the drones attacked. They took on Francis in his palace and lived to tell the tale. They built the hybrid and retrieved the Egg. I think they deserve our trust, don't you? If Dree says we need to wait to attack, then you had better listen to her." She turned to her husband, her hands planted firmly on her hips. She gave him a dark look. "Do you understand me, Abelard Reiter?"

Abelard looked at his wife for a moment, sighed, and then turned back to Dree and Marcus.

He smiled sadly. "She's right, you know. She usually is. I am proud of you both. You have had to take on far too much in this war, and it isn't over yet. Not by a long shot. I trust you, Dree. Build your new hybrid, but move quickly. You have one week, and then we attack, with or without the weapon."

Dree nodded and turned to Marcus.

"If we want to live past next week, we had better get to work."

Chapter 14

Dree blinked against a shower of sparks, carefully watching the seam of the metal as she welded a hulking, angular black wing onto Teen Hybrid. She moved the torch slowly along the joints, always in complete control, even though she was terribly anxious to finish. It had already been three days since she had convinced her father to postpone the attack, and she still had a long way to go.

Teen Hybrid currently looked like some nightmarish specter. Its main hull was still exposed, allowing Jack and Marcus to tinker with the insides, and it only had one clawed hand and the wing that Dree was currently attaching on its right side. A headless neck stretched out to her left, while a huge pile of scrap metal sat behind her. Dree had known almost immediately that Teen Hybrid wouldn't be as powerful as the original: They had fewer drone components, armor plating, and missiles. But they did have the power of the Egg, so that would have to be enough. Dree knew that the main job of this hybrid would be to knock out its predecessor. With Baby Hybrid leading the fleet of drones, the dragons would be severely outmatched.

She glanced over to see Marcus hunched in the corner with a computer core, working on some of the programming. Jack was halfway inside the hull of the hybrid, his legs sticking out comically behind him as he fixed the wiring. She heard him cursing under his breath the whole time.

"If only I had a lab.

"How can I use magic to power a machine?

"A hybrid—how do I get involved with these things?

"I'm going to punch George next time I see him.

"Ow! That's hot!"

Dree just giggled and went back to work. When she finished the weld, she extinguished the torch and stepped back, admiring her work. The new lines were clean and smooth, and the wing would be able to handle the strain of aerial maneuvers. She just wished she could put extra armor plating on the joint like she had last time; well-placed bullets would be able to tear through that weld all too quickly.

She sighed. They'd just have to make do with what they had.

Jack emerged from the hybrid, looking exhausted. His thinning blond-gray hair was plastered to his face with sweat, and the heavy bags under his eyes reached almost to his sharp nose. Like Marcus and Dree, he had barely slept in the last three days. Meanwhile, Lourdvang was curled up in the corner like a massive black cat, snoring loud enough to shake the entire cavern. Dree wished she could go and lie down next to him.

But there just wasn't time. Without Teen Hybrid, the Resistance was badly outgunned.

"How's it going over there?" Jack called to Marcus.

Marcus looked up, the dark circles under his eyes making him look like a raccoon. "All right," he said. "Making a couple of small tweaks. Making sure all the drone AI is offline from Francis's control room."

"That would be ideal," Dree agreed, turning back to the pile of metal. "On to the next wing."

"I think we can afford a small break," Jack said. "Before we all pass out and hurt ourselves."

Dree wanted to argue, but she knew Jack was right. She reluctantly nodded and put down the welding torch. "Just a quick nap."

"Agreed," Jack said, moving wearily to the corner where they had created small beds of excess clothes and packs. Almost the minute his head hit the pillow, his entire body went limp, and he started to snore.

Dree smiled and shook her head. "Poor guy."

Marcus stretched and started for his own makeshift bed, which was set up next to Dree's. They both lay down and stared up at the ominous stalactites that hung over their heads like dragon teeth.

"Do you think we'll finish the hybrid in time?" Marcus asked.

"We have to."

"You know it's not going to be as strong as last time," Marcus said.

"We have the Egg. It'll have to be enough."

"Yeah . . . it cost us enough to get it," Marcus said quietly.

Dree rolled over and looked at Marcus. His chestnut hair was standing on end as usual, and his glasses were fogged over with perspiration.

"You're not responsible for what happened to your dad, you know."

Marcus was quiet for a moment. "I could have gone back for him."

"No," she said. "You couldn't have. They would have captured you too, and then your father's sacrifice would have been for nothing. You did what you had to do. You're here, you're fighting."

"Doesn't feel like it."

"It will," Dree said sadly. "We're just in a holding pattern now, but the battle is coming."

Marcus nodded and then glanced at her. "Yeah. But there's been something else on my mind too."

"What's that?"

He turned back toward the ceiling. "My father invented and built these drones for a reason: to kill the dragons. He wanted vengeance on Helvath, but the red dragons weren't his only target. And maybe he was blinded by rage, and maybe he regrets what he did, but does it really matter? Isn't he just as bad as Francis? Francis is our enemy, but maybe George is actually the villain in all of this."

Dree looked at him for a moment. "I admit . . . I've thought that about him before. I thought about it the day we rescued him, and many times after that. I . . . I couldn't like him."

Marcus nodded, even though the revelation stung.

"Your father destroyed the Dragon Riders," Dree said. "Whether it was his intention or not, he did it. And nothing is going to change that fact. But *you* didn't create these problems. It's not your fault."

"He's still my father, Dree. We share the same blood. I can't just quit on him."

"No, of course not. And maybe he was the villain before, but he's not anymore. He's trying to set it right. He got us the Egg and even sacrificed himself in the process. And I believe in redemption, Marcus. It doesn't change the past, but maybe it can change us. Do you really believe that we can't erase our past sins?"

"I don't know. Maybe some sins are too big to erase."

Dree smiled and then rolled away again, facing Teen Hybrid.

"Maybe you're right," she said, thinking of a fire and a boy with yellow hair. "But I don't think so. We can dwell on the past, Marcus, but I don't think we should. Someone once told me that you have to let go. That means we keep moving . . . and we try to forgive. I haven't mastered that yet, but the time will come when I can forgive your dad. And so will you."

Marcus glanced at her. "And Francis?"

Dree's smile slipped away. "Like I said . . . I haven't mastered it yet. For Francis, I will gladly make an exception."

Dree lay there for a long time, listening to Marcus's gentle breathing. But try as she might, she couldn't fall asleep. She slowly got up and snuck from the cavern, heading into Forost's ever-winding passages to a small chamber where the human refugees were huddled together in the dark. There was no night and day in the mountain, and people slept and woke at random times. She knew many longed for sunlight.

Dree walked into the chamber, lit faintly by a few candles and torches. She spotted her family in the corner: Abi, Rochin, Marny, and Otto, with her mother watching over them like a sentry. Her father wasn't there—he was likely in the war room, planning the attack. He slept even less than Dree did.

Dree wandered over and saw that Abi and the boys were asleep. Rochin was sitting up, hugging his knees and staring at nothing. He had been helping with the armor a little, but mostly he just sat and slept and stared. He looked bad too—pale skin and gaunt features, like he was quickly becoming a ghost.

"Dree?" her mother said, looking over. "Hey."

"Hey, Mom," Dree said. "Can we talk?"

Her mother nodded and stood up. "What's wrong?"

"Let's walk for a second."

Dree took her mother's hand and led her from the chamber, not wanting anyone else to overhear. She could feel Rochin's eyes on her back, but she ignored him. She needed to talk to her mother alone.

"What's wrong?" her mother asked, sounding worried.

Dree stopped and faced her, and for the second time in a week, her eyes filled with tears.

"I started that house fire when we were kids," she said coarsely, her voice breaking. "I didn't mean to. My . . . my skin causes them sometimes. Like Eria said back in the war room. I think I'm a Fury. I can't control it. When I'm angry or upset . . . the flames just come to the surface. And I was mad. I was mad you sent me up to my room, and I sat there and it started to get warm. I didn't even know what was happening. The fire was already raging when I realized. I didn't even feel it. That's when it all began. The screaming. I did it, Mom. You were right. I caused the house fire. I'm responsible for Gavri's death."

Dree's mother put a trembling hand to her mouth, as if disbelieving, and soon tears were streaming down her face as well. Dree expected her mother to scream, to slap her, to storm off back to the chamber and never speak to her again. Instead, she wrapped Dree in a hug, pulling her into the nook of her shoulder.

"It wasn't your fault, Dree. Even when I suspected you had done something and I said those things . . . I knew it wasn't your fault. You were a child and you didn't know any better. And now . . . now that I know this. I am so sorry, Dree. I was so broken . . . so sad . . . I needed to blame someone. Anyone. And I blamed you, because I knew something had happened, even if I didn't know what. It was wrong. I am so sorry."

They held each other for a while, and Dree let the tears spill out. Her mother pulled back.

"You are not responsible," she said firmly, taking Dree's face in her hands. "You are a Fury, and you were far too young to control your powers. It is not your fault. Do you understand?"

Dree nodded, almost unable to see through her tears. "I saw him. I was falling from Baby Hybrid, and I was about to die. I thought maybe I deserved it. And . . . Gavri came to me on the back of a dragon, and he told me that I wasn't done here yet. He looked so happy. He was just like I remembered, Mom."

Her mom started to cry again, and they embraced. Finally Dree led her mother back to their family, where Rochin still watched them carefully, and then Dree started back for Marcus and the others.

She climbed onto her makeshift bed and slipped into a peaceful sleep.

When they woke, work immediately started again. Hours melted by with the flame of the torch and the slow, meticulous wiring of the hull. Lourdvang woke up and began to help as well, carting over the heavier pieces of metal and breathing fire onto the metal when Dree's torch wasn't hot enough. Marcus and Jack worked side by side, finishing the extremely complicated casings for the power cells and twin computer cores.

Dree had moved on to the second wing now, welding hinges and joints to allow the hybrid to maneuver more effectively—she was trying everything she could to give it any advantage over the original. Propulsion engines were fixed to the back of each wing as before, and she had attached two machine guns under each wing as well. The new hybrid was starting to take shape, but it still had a long way to go.

Jack suddenly threw down a wrench. "Impossible," he said. "It doesn't make sense!"

"What?" Marcus asked, peering out from farther down the hull.

"The power cell transfer," Jack said, staring at the hybrid. "I've been thinking about it for days now. We just don't have the conduits necessary. You can't just transfer kinetic energy into metal, Marcus. You can't move legs without hydraulics, and we don't have them. None of this is even possible!"

Marcus exchanged a look with Dree. He climbed out of the hull and nodded at Lourdvang.

"That's because you're thinking with normal physics," Marcus said.

Jack frowned. "As opposed to . . . ?"

"Well, you're in Dracone. Teen Hybrid isn't purely mechanical. Lourdvang?"

Lourdvang bent down and breathed a small plume of fire into the wing, the flames flowing over the pistons and joints and gears. The wing suddenly moved upward, as if alive, and the circuitry hummed to life.

"How?" Jack whispered.

"It's an energy source," Marcus explained, "like the Egg. Magic is real here. But really, what is magic anyway? I figure it's just everything normal science can't explain. That doesn't mean it isn't real."

Jack stared at him. "You've grown up fast, Mr. Brimley."

Marcus shrugged. "A dragon–drone war will do that to you."

Jack smiled, and they both climbed back into the skeletal hull. Dree resumed her welding, creating a new bead around some reinforced steel plating. The metal bubbled and merged, forging a new, stronger bond. Lourdvang curled up behind her, watching the wing slowly take shape.

"I might say the same for you," Lourdvang said, eyeing her as she moved on to another section. "You've matured a great deal since all of this began."

"And you, baby brother."

He chuckled, spewing a wave of black smoke. "All of us, I guess. I feel as old as stone."

Dree glanced at him. "You're becoming the leader you were meant to be."

"Meant to be? I'm an abandoned orphan," he pointed out. "I was meant to be dead."

"If that were true, I wouldn't have found you. You're the son of Erdath now. The future leader of the Nightwings."

Lourdvang blinked one giant blue eye and shook his head, a gesture she had taught him.

"That was never decided."

Dree shrugged and turned back to her welding. "We don't get to decide our fate."

"I think you're deciding your fate right now."

Dree laughed. "You're probably right. Can you grab me another plate, baby brother?"

"If I'm going to be the leader of the Nightwings, you're going to have to stop calling me that."

"Never."

Lourdvang snorted and went to retrieve another metal plate. For just a moment, it felt like they were all at peace. But Dree knew the war was still waiting. That people and dragons were dying with every passing hour, and that Francis was still after them. Her smile slipped away, and she got back to work.

A few days later, Dree, Marcus, Abelard, Nathaniel, and Erdath sat together in the empty war room, all of them looking grim. The week was all too quickly drawing to a close, and the attack was nearing. Teen Hybrid had finally taken shape in a haze of fire and circuitry, and she would be ready. Barely.

"The palace is well protected," Nathaniel said. "But not invulnerable."

Marcus shook his head. "They will have installed defenses in the water and sewage systems after our last break-in. And if there are drones hovering overhead, it will be a bloody battle to get past them."

"My scouts say that there are at least ten drones overhead at all times," Erdath said.

Abelard looked at him, shaking his head. "And many more a short flight away."

"I agree it would be better to get in quietly," Dree said, "but it just won't be possible this time. The drones have infrared and radar, and they don't need to sleep. Does Francis ever leave the palace?"

"No," Nathaniel said. "Never. We have a few spies in the city keeping watch. They are all instructed to take a shot at him if they can, but they don't get the chance. He's much too careful now."

"Take a shot?" Dree asked. "Is this an assassination now?"

Abelard and Nathaniel exchanged a look. "If need be," Abelard said.

Erdath growled, and Dree gave her father a cool look. "Even if he deserves it, I thought we said we were going to be better than our enemies? How does an assassination make us any better than Xidorne?"

"We are going to try to take him alive," Abelard said. "And put him on trial. But if we can't—"

"He dies," Nathaniel finished coolly. "And the war is over."

Marcus and Dree exchanged a glance, but Dree knew there was no use in arguing. "Fine."

"So if we can't sneak in, we have to press a full attack," Marcus reasoned, staring at the map of the palace. "But it will have to be lightning quick. If the full drone army gets there, we'll be wiped out."

"What about this precious hybrid?" Nathaniel asked scornfully.

"It will help," Dree said. "With the Egg, the new hybrid will be very powerful. But things can happen in battle. It could malfunction, or the Egg could be knocked out of its power casing by bullets or missiles. We can't rely on it alone."

"Agreed," Abelard said. "A full attack is our only chance. Teen Hybrid will lead the aerial attack, escorted by every dragon we can put in the mix. They need to win the skies quickly. We will have armored fighters dropped over the walls—we have about nine fire-resistant suits so far we can use. Nathaniel and I will be among them."

"And so will we," Dree cut in.

Abelard paused. "I would really prefer if you stayed—"

"We've been in the palace before," Marcus said. "And we

don't need armor. You're going to need our help. Dree will be riding on Teen Hybrid, and I'll come in with Lourdvang."

Abelard looked at his daughter and then sighed, as if sensing her resolve. "Very well. We get in, we grab Francis and take the control room. As soon as we have that, we can shut down the drones. The war will be over. The Resistance will resume control of the city, and we can put Francis on trial." He turned to Erdath. "All dragon hunting will cease, and Dragon Riders will once again protect the land."

Erdath nodded. "A good dream. But first we must get to Xidorne and the control room."

"We leave in two days," Abelard said. He turned to Dree. "Make sure the hybrid is ready."

Dree and Marcus left the meeting and started back for their cavern. They climbed the sloping tunnels, their shoes scraping against the rock. Voices from the war room followed them as they walked.

"They have a real thing about leaving us out of the planning," Marcus said sourly.

"I noticed that," Dree replied.

"Hey!" a voice called out behind them.

They looked back to find Ciaran Rose hurrying up behind them, her raven hair tied back in a long braid. As always, she looked ready for war: She wore a brown leather jerkin, gauntlets, and her long sword.

"Marcus. Dree. We haven't had much chance to talk," Ciaran said. "Walk with me?"

"Sure," Marcus replied.

Ciaran led them down the tunnel, silent for a moment. Then she turned to them.

"It's amazing . . . two Furies at once. Nathaniel told me what happened in the factory."

Marcus shifted. "I lost control."

"You showed your power." She suddenly stopped and faced them. "It's a dangerous thing."

"We'll be fine," Dree said, annoyed. This was none of Ciaran's business.

Ciaran met her eyes. "My mother was a Rider."

"I know," Dree said. "I'm sorry to hear she passed."

"She was murdered," Ciaran said coolly. "By Dareon the Black."

Marcus and Dree exchanged a look. "I'm sorry," Dree said.

"He killed ten Riders before they stopped him," she said. "Imagine what two Furies could do."

"We're not like that," Marcus said, flushing. "We would never hurt another Rider."

"I hope you're right," Ciaran said. She looked away. "You've done nothing wrong. I just . . . am troubled by the fact that the Furies have returned. I've been waiting my whole life to be a Dragon Rider. Hiding my family history in the shadows and pretending to be a normal girl at school. When I was thirteen I joined the Resistance, and we plotted for some way to end Francis's hold on the city. Finally, the war has come. And now . . . you are here."

"What do you mean?" Marcus asked.

She paused. "I just want to make sure we don't replace Francis with something worse."

Dree laughed, too stunned to do anything else. "You think we want to rule Dracone?"

"I think you have the potential to."

Dree shook her head. "I want peace, Ciaran. And I want to be a Dragon Rider like my father. I spent my whole life hiding my true identity too. Living in the docks, poor as dirt, and barely having enough to eat, even though I *knew* what I could do." She felt her temper rising again, and her voice got louder. "Not to mention I love the dragons as much as anyone. I raised Lourdvang from a baby. You and I have the same dream. And I don't need you questioning who I am . . . or Marcus, for that matter. Do you understand?"

Ciaran studied Dree for a moment, scanning over her critically.

"I think we might just become friends, Driele Reiter."

Dree opened her mouth to retort, and then frowned, surprised.

"Oh. Well, I hope so," Dree said.

"You've got fire, that's for sure," Ciaran said. "But I'm glad you're on my side."

She stuck out a hand, and Dree gripped it firmly. The two girls nodded at each other.

"I also don't want to rule," Marcus added, poking his head in between them.

Dree snorted. "Thanks, Marcus. See you around, Ciaran."

"I look forward to it, Furies."

She stalked back down the tunnel, and Marcus glanced at Dree. "That was odd."

"It seems that Furies make people nervous."

"It makes me nervous too sometimes."

The two of them started walking again. Dree glanced at him, raising an eyebrow.

"You are as red as Helvath."

"I am not."

"You're as bad as Brian."

They reached their workshop cavern, where the nearly complete Teen Hybrid sat in the middle of the room, facing the entrance. She had both wings now and even a formed head, along with three of four limbs. Jack was still working on some of the wiring, and he didn't even notice them come in.

"Think she will win this war for us?" Marcus asked, eyeing the machine guns.

Dree nodded. "She'll help. Not bad for a week's work. I'm going to put the last leg on—"

She was interrupted by a massive boom that shook the ground beneath them, echoing through the caves like thunder. Dree nearly stumbled, just barely catching herself, and then looked at Marcus.

This explosion was not like the ones before.

This one had come from inside the caverns.

Chapter 15

Marcus and Dree sprinted downward through the tunnels, and they heard shouting and the deep grumble of dragons' voices coming from all sides as everyone converged on the noise. Marcus struggled to keep up with the fleet-footed Dree, feeling his sides burning with a cramp. They turned the corner into another large open chamber, and both of them slid to a halt.

"Rochin?" Dree whispered.

Her brother was standing in the middle of the cavern, a strange weapon perched on his shoulder. It looked like some sort of crude rocket launcher—a gleaming black metal chamber and a two-foot barrel that extended out in front of him like the gun of a tank. And there, sitting in the weapon's open chamber, was the Egg, pulsating with red-and-orange fire and filling the rocket launcher with its deadly energy.

But that wasn't the worst of it.

About fifty feet away, lying on the ground, was Vero. A great, charred hole had been blasted into the crimson scales on her chest, and she was motionless, her wings spread out limply across the cavern.

Dree rushed forward and snatched the Egg out of Rochin's weapon, turning away from him and cradling it. Marcus could see the rage in her eyes as she turned back, and little flames played on her skin.

"What is this?" she demanded.

Rochin backed away. "She . . . she attacked. I had to stop her."

"Where did you get that gun?" She clenched her fist and took a step toward him. "Francis?"

Rochin was still backing away. "He told me . . . if I got the Egg . . . you would all be spared. He was going to name me to the Ruling Council. There's no hope for us, Dree. It was my chance to be something."

"You betrayed your own family?" Dree asked, shaking.

Marcus walked up behind her, feeling her tangible anger. Rochin was still backing away.

"Help," Vero moaned, her voice cracking and soft.

Dree and Marcus glanced over and saw that the red dragon was trying to get up but couldn't. Without thinking, both of them rushed over to help. Marcus looked at the injury—it was far worse than Emmett's.

"Stay still," Marcus said. "You've been injured."

"Yes," she said in her low, gravelly voice. "Fatally, I believe. He . . . he has the Egg. You have to get it back."

"I have it," Dree said. "It's okay."

Behind them, humans and dragons rushed into the room. They heard an awful roar and saw Nolong rush inside, his eyes on Vero. Dree and Marcus stepped back to let him crouch down beside her.

"What happened?" Abelard demanded.

Dree whirled to find her brother, but he was gone. "Rochin," she spat. "He had a weapon. Francis sent him to get the Egg. Vero tried to stop him."

Nolong made a low noise in his throat and tried to breathe his rippling golden fire on the wound.

Vero stopped him. "It's too late," she managed. "In the next life, my love."

Marcus saw the life suddenly drain out of her, and her head fell back. Her great crimson body relaxed on the floor as Nolong closed his eyes and laid his head on hers, silent.

The whole room watched, stunned into silence.

"So many years to find each other again," Nolong said quietly. "And now she is gone."

Marcus felt his eyes well with tears. Sages had a great power to bring joy and peace, but when they suffered, everyone around them could feel it.

Dree turned to Marcus. "We need to find my brother."

Marcus quickly followed her out of the cavern, and they searched through the winding passages, calling out for Rochin. But it was in vain . . . he had likely planned his escape well in advance. Even now he was probably on his way back to Dracone—without the Egg, but with Vero's blood on his hands.

Dree clenched her fists again, letting the fire dance up her arms. "I'm going after him."

"I'll come with you."

"Lourdvang!" she shouted. "We're going!"

They started for the nearest exit from the mountain. Lourdvang and Erdath had shown them the many secret openings that pockmarked Forost like a monstrous honeycomb. When they reached the opening, tucked beneath an overhanging crevice, Lourdvang appeared from another tunnel. He was not alone. Erdath was walking with him, looking solemn. They stepped right in front of Dree and Marcus.

"Leave him," Lourdvang said quietly.

"What?" Dree asked.

"We don't need a prisoner right now. And in your anger, you might do something you regret."

"He killed Vero!" Marcus said.

"Yes," Erdath said. "And he will have to live with that. Let him run with his burden."

Erdath and Lourdvang exchanged a look, and then Lourdvang lowered himself to face them directly.

"This is the influence of the Egg," he said. "It is why Erdath was so worried about our mission to retrieve it. It is too powerful, too unpredictable. Rochin's weapon could never have killed Vero without the Egg's energy. With it, she had no chance."

"That's why we have to use it," Marcus said. "It's the only thing strong enough to stop Francis!"

"And what if Francis gets the Egg?" Erdath asked, looking down at him.

Marcus flushed. "We won't let that happen."

Dree looked at Marcus, hesitating. Marcus scowled. "You agree with them?"

"My brother just killed a massive Flame with the Egg's power. Imagine what Francis could do with it."

Marcus shook his head and turned away. "We need it to win. Ask your father and the other fighters."

"I'm sure they will agree with you," Lourdvang said. "But that doesn't mean they're right."

"This time they are," Marcus said stubbornly.

He couldn't believe they were having this conversation after everything they had gone through to get the Egg. They had nearly been killed in the attempt, and George was now sitting in a CIA cell because of that mission. Not to mention they had just spent the last week building a hybrid that relied on the Egg to have any hope of defeating the drones. They had pinned everything on that hope.

"You're all upset about Vero," Marcus said. "I am too. But we have to stick to the plan."

Dree put a calming hand on Marcus's arm. "Okay. Let's get back to the hybrid."

"We'll talk later," Lourdvang said. "Erdath and I will make sure all our guards are in place."

Dree took Marcus's hand and led him back to the cavern, and Marcus felt better with her familiar, comforting presence next to him. They walked in silence for a while, and Marcus glanced at her.

"Sorry I got a little heated," he murmured.

Dree nodded. "I don't blame you . . . I'm just as angry as you are. My brother is a coward. And Vero . . . she was very brave. It's a terrible loss . . . I just want to make sure there aren't any more of them." When they reached the chamber, she squeezed his hand and turned to go. "I'd better go talk to my mother."

"Good luck," Marcus said, watching her hurry off. The loss of Vero sat deep in his gut.

He joined Jack at the hybrid, and his uncle popped his head out of the hull, covered in grease.

"What was that noise?" he called.

"A traitor," Marcus said quietly. "Rochin was working for Francis."

"What?" Jack said, dropping a tool into the hybrid. "What happened? Are you all right?"

"He almost got the Egg. He . . . he killed Vero. I saw her die. She was trying to get up . . . and Nolong tried, but it was too late."

Jack climbed out of the hull, somber. "I'm sorry to hear that, Marcus."

"She had just found Nolong again. It doesn't seem fair."

Jack put a hand on Marcus's shoulder. "Death doesn't seem to care about what's fair. I was away on a business trip when my mother died. I was always with her before that. I went there every night to bring her dinner, or mow the grass, or just sit and talk. My brother lived far away, and my father was already dead, so I was all she had left. And then I was asked to go overseas for a demonstration. Some new technology I had designed. I didn't want to go, but she told me that my career had to come first. So I left . . . just for a week."

Marcus had never heard him speak of his mother before.

"She died while I was gone," Jack said. "I was heartbroken. I wasn't there for her." He put a hand on Marcus's shoulder. "But life goes on, Marcus. It went on for me. It went on for your father after your mother was killed. And all the death here, everything you've seen, you can't let it stop you."

Marcus looked away. "Sometimes it just seems like too much . . . you know?"

"That's why you have friends," he replied. "And even a tired old uncle."

Marcus smiled. "Thanks. I guess we don't really have time for mourning."

"There will be time. But Vero, your mother, my mother—they would tell us to get to work."

"You're probably right. The battle is drawing closer."

Jack ducked back into the hull. "Then you had better get those machine guns online," he called.

Marcus snorted. "You know, most uncles probably wouldn't encourage that."

"I'm not most uncles. And you're not most nephews."

"Fair enough."

Marcus ducked down to start on the machine gun, connecting the circuitry to the computer core. As he worked, he thought back to his conversation with Dree. Something was nagging at him about it . . . Dree almost never gave up on an argument. In fact, he couldn't remember ever winning one with her. Ever. She was as stubborn as dirt, and yet she had stopped arguing.

Had she been lying to him? No. Dree would never do that. They were a team.

He connected a wire into a power cell, and suddenly the huge, black barrel of the machine gun began to whir. The magazine inside clicked into place. Before Marcus could shout a warning, the gun unloaded a hail of bullets into the cavern wall, biting deep into the rock. Jack ducked in alarm and fell off the side of the hybrid, covering his head.

Marcus quickly pulled out the wire, and the machine gun fell silent.

He stared at it, stunned. "I think I'd better program that computer core first."

Jack stood up again, rubbing his tailbone and scowling. "Good idea."

Chapter 16

Lourdvang soared over the Teeth, the craggy, snow-blasted peaks reaching up toward his wings like grasping claws. They were flying dangerously low—just over the mountains or dropping into the valleys and twisting through the range, riding air currents and sending the surviving birds scattering.

Dree knew they had to try to stay out of view of any Flames for as long as possible. They needed to speak to Helvath directly—and he might have given orders to kill her and Lourdvang on sight. He had let them go last time, but he had been very clear that they were never to return, and while Dree now knew that she was likely immune to Helvath's flames, the enormous dragon would have no problem tearing her apart.

A satchel was tucked over Dree's shoulder, flapping in the wind, and there was a very valuable piece of cargo inside. In fact, that cargo was their only chance for leaving this place alive. She knew Marcus would be furious, but she also knew he would never agree to give up the Egg. Neither would her father or Nathaniel. But Erdath and Lourdvang were right: They were dragons, after all, and they understood better than anyone the power and danger of the Egg. It was a power that humans had no right to wield. She shuddered to think what would have happened if Rochin had managed to get the Egg back to Francis.

The Egg had to go back where it belonged . . . where only Marcus's father had ever managed to get his hands on it.

It had to go to Arncrag, the home of the Flames.

"We're taking a big risk going to see him again," Lourdvang said, not for the first time.

He had wanted to send Teen Hybrid to deliver it, or take it himself. But Teen Hybrid wasn't ready to fly yet, and Dree wasn't about to let Lourdvang go alone. So here they were.

"I know. But I think the Egg should keep him calm. Besides, Helvath deserves to know about Vero."

Lourdvang snarled. "If he hadn't exiled her, she'd still be alive."

"And Francis would have the Egg," Dree pointed out. "She stopped Rochin, Lourdvang. Don't let her death be in vain."

Lourdvang paused. "We're getting close."

Dree looked up and saw Arncrag rising out of the mono-lithic Teeth—the tallest of all the mountains. It looked to have been carved by wind and flame, jagged and sharp like a much-used fang, its soaring peak rising almost to the clouds. She tightened her hold a little on Lourdvang's scales. She had almost been killed twice at Arncrag already. Maybe three times really was pushing their luck.

"We have company," Lourdvang muttered.

Two massive Flames, each of them twice the size of Lourdvang, had taken off from their posts on the tops of two other mountains. They swept toward them instantly, flanking them on either side.

"You are trespassing," one of them growled. "Why are you here?"

"We wish to speak to Helvath," Lourdvang called out. "We have a gift for him."

The dragon laughed—a low, cruel sound. "It had better be a good one. He is hungry lately."

The two dragons guided them to the great entrance of Arncrag, and Lourdvang landed gently on the barren out-cropping. Dree hopped off, and together they walked under the towering archway, still flanked by the two sentries. The Flames stopped at the opening, and Lourdvang and Dree entered alone.

Helvath was sitting on his massive stone dais. His great black claws were wrapped around the front of the dais, and his equally black eyes—looking as malicious and hungry as ever—watched as Lourdvang and Dree entered. To his left sat the smaller, pinkish female dragon, whom Dree recognized from the last time they had visited Helvath. That dragon had always seemed even crueller than Helvath. Dree tried not to tremble as they approached the dais.

"You two are tempting fate," Helvath boomed. "Twice I have let you live, when my laws are clear: Enter these lands and die. But a third time? Now you have gone too far, worm and his Rider."

Lourdvang bristled, but Dree laid a calming hand on his side.

"We have come for a good reason," Dree said.

Helvath smiled, flames licking out through his teeth. "I hope so. I am ever so hungry of late. Those machines are chasing away much of my dinner. Was I not just saying that, Vicar?"

The smaller, pinkish dragon stared at Dree. "I believe you were."

Dree swung her satchel around and quickly removed the Egg. Helvath straightened.

"I offer you a gift," she said. "The return of the Egg to its rightful home."

Helvath looked at her carefully, his great black eyes betraying nothing. Then he extended a large, clawed hand toward her, and she put the Egg in his scaled palm. She saw radiant fire leap from the Egg, as if awakened by his touch. There were a few other Flames standing in the shadows, and she saw them all watching in fascination. Their growling voices echoed around the room.

Helvath stared at the Egg for a long time, closing his hand on it. Fire crept through his fingers.

"Where did you find it?" he said, almost in a whisper.

"The man who stole it hid it in another world. I went there and got it back."

Helvath eyed Dree suspiciously. "And you offer it to me, despite its obvious power. Why?"

Dree met his fierce gaze. "Because we have seen that power, and also the harm it can do. It is not right for us to use it, and I have to make sure it doesn't fall into Francis's hands. I trust that you will keep it safe."

Helvath thought about that for a moment and then nodded.

"This is a worthy gift, young Rider. Enough that I will let you leave unscathed. Now go."

Dree didn't move. "There is more. Vero is dead . . . killed by someone using the Egg."

Helvath and Vicar both immediately stood straighter, gnashing their teeth. "Dead?"

"Yes. The enemy that we face is strong. Strong enough even to kill a Flame like Vero. We need your help, Helvath. We need the Flames for the coming war. If you don't help us, we are going to be outmatched. And don't be foolish—once the drones are done with us, you'll be next. Francis will turn his army on you as well. By helping us stop them, you protect yourselves too. *Please*."

Dree heard some of the other Flames muttering again, including Vicar, and she saw them all looking at Helvath, who seemed to be taking stock of Dree. He flexed his clawed hands, clearly distraught by the news of Vero's death, and for a moment she thought he might agree to help them fight.

But once again, she was wrong.

"No," Helvath said at last. "The Flames do not concern themselves with the trials of lower creatures. It is your war, and Vero should never have gotten herself involved. We will take care of ourselves, Reiter. The Egg will be safe here, I promise you that. Now both of you go, before you test my patience further still. For this gift you have safe passage and nothing more. Go fight your little war."

Dree slumped, defeated. They couldn't rely on the Flames, and the Egg was gone.

They were truly on their own.

"Fair enough," she said quietly.

She walked out with Lourdvang and climbed onto his back.

"We did the right thing," he said softly.

"I know," she said. "But it certainly doesn't feel like it."

He stepped off the ledge, catching a wind current and sailing into the air. "Now what?"

"Now we think of a new plan. And fast."

Chapter 17

Marcus finished wiring the holding chamber for the Egg and stood back, admiring their creation. He had created three extra power conduits to allow for the massive energy expelled by the Egg, and it looked like it would work—though it was hard to calculate the exact metrics of an ancient magical relic. The hybrid was now ready to go— once Dree welded the last leg on, they could put it through some tests.

"Looks pretty good!" Jack said, standing behind Marcus with his arms folded over his chest.

They had been disturbed a few hours earlier by yet another drone attack—once again, the mountain had shaken and rock had come loose, sending them running for shelter, but thankfully no one had been hurt. Marcus suspected the drones were testing the mountain for weaknesses or trying to draw the fighters out. It had lasted only for ten or twenty minutes—just enough to get everyone nervous.

"We'll just have to hope it's enough," Marcus replied, glancing at his uncle.

Jack looked exhausted—his eyes were bloodshot and he hadn't washed in a week—but there was definite satisfaction on his face when he looked at the hybrid. They had worked almost nonstop for the entire week, sleeping just a few hours a night, but they had created something that might just help to win the war. If the Egg performed like they hoped, even the drones would have trouble keeping up with Teen Hybrid. Marcus envisioned himself riding into battle, fast as lightning.

"I still think I should be going with you guys."

"You're not a fighter," Marcus reminded him.

"And you are?"

Marcus laughed. "No. Not really. But I am a Dragon Rider. That counts for something."

"Yes, it does. I always wondered about that Xbox you burned to a heap of plastic."

"Bet you're regretting adopting a freak, huh?"

Jack turned to him, smiling. "Never. I adopted the best kid I know. And now he's turning into one of the best *men* I know. Your father has made many mistakes, Marcus, but you are not one of them."

"Thanks," Marcus said, feeling his cheeks burning. "And he made the right call leaving me with you."

Suddenly, they heard footsteps. Marcus turned, relieved to have an interruption, and saw Dree and Lourdvang enter the cavern. Dree looked a bit sheepish, and Lourdvang kept his eyes on the hybrid, examining its progress.

"Where were you?" Marcus demanded, looking between them.

Dree didn't meet his eyes. "I had to do something."

"We were attacked again a few hours ago, and we couldn't find you. We were worried sick."

"We saw the damage," Dree replied. "The skies were clear when we got back, though."

Marcus folded his arms across his chest. "Back from where?"

"Nowhere—" Dree started, trying to push past him.

"Dree."

She met his eyes coolly. "I brought the Egg back to Helvath."

Even though Marcus had feared the worst, he was still shocked by Dree's admission. He instantly felt his temper rising. They were supposed to be a *team*, and she hadn't even consulted him.

"How could you do that?" Marcus yelled.

"We had to! Humans were never meant to have that kind of dragon magic, Marcus. We—"

"We almost died getting that Egg!" Marcus cut in, fuming. "Do you remember? My father is sitting in a prison cell right now because of that Egg. And you gave it away without even telling me? You had no right!"

"No *right*?" Dree snapped. Her eyes started to flash orange and crimson. "I had *every* right!"

"Dree," Lourdvang said, trying to calm her.

"No," Dree said, waving him away. "I don't have to listen to you lecture me, Marcus. You've been in Dracone for, what, a few weeks? And you think you know everything? Like you're some sort of expert on *my* home? What do you know about this world? What do you know about dragon magic and its real power?"

"I know that we needed that Egg to beat Francis."

Dree narrowed her eyes. "You don't think I want to beat him? He destroyed my home. He killed my neighbors and friends. He broke my father's spine. *Mine.* You might have been born here, but you are not *from* here. You don't know our history. You've barely experienced our way of life. You don't belong here, Marcus. I told you that back on Earth—where your father is waiting for you. The man who did all this, by the way. Your father brought the drones to this world and started this whole war. So why don't you stop helping, Marcus, and just go back home? We don't need you."

The venom in her words caused Marcus to step back, and Dree immediately softened.

"I'm sorry . . . I didn't . . . I mean, you're not . . . I'm just frustrated—"

"At least I know where you stand," Marcus said, before storming out of the cavern. If she didn't want his help, that was fine. He didn't need her either. He had been working alone since he was a little kid.

He would take care of this war himself.

Marcus made his way quickly through the mountains, holding the collar of his jacket to his chin to block out the cold. He had descended Forost under cover of darkness, his eyes always peeled for drones. But the night skies were clear, twinkling only with the pale light of the stars, and Marcus made it to the relative safety of the valley undetected. He had been walking through the woods for hours now. His feet ached with every step on the soil, but he had to get to the city.

Marcus knew he could never get the Egg now. Not from Helvath. The old dragon would have it guarded day and night, and no human or dragon would get near Arncrag again without being detected.

But he could do the next best thing and get his hands on Rochin's weapon. George must have created the launcher while working for Francis—it was too advanced to be Draconian technology. While the launcher would be much weaker without the Egg, it could still be used to blow through the palace wall, or at least take down some drones. It alone wouldn't win the war, but at least it would give Marcus some sort of advantage.

And most important, he wanted to get the weapon out of Francis's hands.

Maybe when Marcus had taken down the palace walls himself, Dree would realize that Marcus cared about Dracone just as much as she did.

He felt heat coursing through him at the thought of their fight. How could Dree have dismissed Marcus like that after everything they had been through? After everything he had done? They had fought side by side. They were *friends*. At least, Marcus thought they were friends.

But maybe he was wrong. His veins ran with the same blood as his father—the blood of a murderer. Dree had said herself that she couldn't forgive Marcus's father. Maybe she hadn't forgiven Marcus for that connection either. On Earth, Marcus was always known as the son of a traitor—maybe he was a fool to think it would be any different in Dracone.

His eyes were suddenly thick with tears, and he roughly wiped them on his sleeve. It didn't matter now. Only stopping Francis mattered. And getting Rochin's weapon was a start.

Of course, the whole plan was pretty close to madness. Even in his stubborn mind-set, Marcus knew that. He had no idea where Rochin had gone, other than that he was likely hiding somewhere in the city. He might have already returned the weapon, but Marcus was hoping that his guilt and fear over not getting the Egg had him worried about returning to Francis. Maybe he was waiting for another shot.

Marcus was banking on that possibility.

Soon the lights of the city appeared before him, and he made his way across the meadow toward the outskirts. Even the butterflies had abandoned the tall grass now, and it looked ghostly and barren in the light of the moon. He walked among the ruins, lit only by the campfires of the survivors still living in the shattered remainders of their homes. His heart felt heavy at the reminder of the death and destruction.

He thought back to Dree's words. His father had been the cause of all this. It made Marcus feel ill. Could a good person truly create this much evil?

He picked up a doll—half-burned and thick with ash. It crumbled away in his hand.

Marcus was so much like George. They had the same interests, the same skills. They even looked the same. If George was capable of fostering such destruction, was Marcus capable of doing the same thing?

As Marcus wandered into the city proper, he saw the taller buildings at the center, still untouched by war. They were gleaming and clean, looking down on the destruction around them. Marcus felt his anger rising, so he kept moving. He passed brick houses and quaint shops, all still standing, and saw people milling about, either up early or out late. A bustling tavern stood at the end of the street, and a mob of drunk men stood in front of it. Marcus hurried past them, not wanting to draw any attention to himself.

It didn't work.

"Hey!" a voice rang out.

Marcus turned and saw an armed soldier step out from the crowd, wobbling and clearly drunk. He was wearing the gleaming black fire-resistant armor of the Protectorate, and he had his right hand on his spear.

He started for Marcus, recognition in his watery eyes. "Stop!"

Marcus ignored him and kept walking, but the man grabbed his arm and spun him around.

"The glasses," he said softly. "I remember you from the palace. You're a rebel!"

He went for his spear, and Marcus pushed him away, trying to wriggle free from his grasp. He got his arm loose and turned to run, but the soldier grabbed him again and wrestled him to the ground.

"Let me go!" Marcus shouted, writhing like a fish on a line.

"You're going to the Prime Minister," the soldier said, his breath rank with beer. "Alive or dead . . . it doesn't matter to me, boy! Someone go grab another Protectorate patrol! Tell them I've caught a rebel!"

Marcus felt his heat rising as the man pinned his arms, trying to keep him down.

"I'm warning you . . . let me go!" Marcus said, his whole body shaking now.

The soldier laughed. "Or what?"

Marcus closed his eyes. He was still afraid of what he was capable of, but he couldn't allow himself to be captured.

Not now. The fire raced through him, as if a dam had come crashing down, and the soldier suddenly screamed. He let go of Marcus and backed away, trying to slap out the fire that had caught on his sleeves.

"What did you do?" he said, slurring his words. "Someone get help! Hurry!"

"I told you to leave me alone!" Marcus shouted, all of the anger and frustration of the last few weeks bubbling to the surface at once. This time, he felt *power.* Intoxicating, burning power.

Without thinking, he turned and stretched his right arm out. A sizzling fireball erupted from his hand, orange and yellow and about the size of a basketball. It whizzed past the ducking soldier's head and hit the tavern full on, exploding like a comet. Fire spread over the building in waves, and the crowd of drinkers screamed and took off running. The patrons inside followed suit, streaming out of the tavern.

The soldier took another look at Marcus, his face white, and then he ran off.

Marcus watched them all go, their screams echoing behind them. The tavern was fully ablaze now, lighting up the night. Marcus looked down at his hands. What had he done? What was he becoming?

He remembered the story of Dareon. Were all Furies evil? Was he?

Was he even worse than his father?

All at once, the fire inside Marcus died down, but the tavern was still consumed by flames. Marcus was about to go try to help put out the fire when he felt a strong hand on his shoulder. He turned and found Abelard looking at him, his expression grim.

"We're leaving," he said. "Now."

Chapter 18

Dree sat alone in the cavern, perched on the hybrid's wing. Her stomach felt like it was alive, roiling and turning and refusing to let her get back to work. Lourdvang had left to keep the skies clear for her father, who had gone after Marcus alone. Abelard had told her to sit tight and cool off, and somehow she had actually agreed.

Now Marcus *and* her father were in danger. Guilt gnawed at Dree.

She remembered the look on Marcus's face when she told him to go home and that he didn't belong in Dracone. How could she have said that to him? Her stomach churned at the thought of it. She knew that she had struck deep—

both with that comment and the one about his father. She knew how embarrassed he was about his father's creation of the drones, and how Marcus felt like he was responsible too. It was a terrible thing to say to him. She knew as well as anyone how it felt to be ashamed of a father.

But even that had changed. Abelard was no longer a shadow on a chair. He had become what Dree had always hoped he would—the Rider, the hero, the leader. She had dreamed of him returning to his calling since she was a little girl. And now that he had . . . was she truly happy about it? It was great that he was leading the army. For all of Dree's efforts, she didn't want to be responsible for the Resistance too. They needed someone older, someone with more experience. Abelard was perfect for the job.

But as the Resistance leader, he was also putting himself in danger. She had just gotten him back, and now he was flying into battle. A selfish part of her wasn't ready for that either.

Now that he had finally become the man she knew he could be, she realized she wanted her dad more than she wanted a hero after all. She didn't want to lose him again.

And she didn't want to lose Marcus either.

She wondered if some of her anger was just fear. Maybe it was why she had tried to leave Marcus back on Earth, after she had retrieved the Egg. She didn't want to give *him* the choice, because she was afraid he would choose to leave. It had been that way her whole life—people choosing to leave her. Her mother had ignored her for years after the fire. Her father had drifted away soon after. Rochin had left the family for something he thought was better, and Wilhelm had sent her into the streets. Almost everyone she knew had chosen to leave her at some point. And more than once, she had wondered if she was the cause—if she drove people away, and if, one day, Lourdvang and Abi might leave her too.

"Dree?" a voice said.

She looked up and saw Nathaniel walk into the cavern, his sword dangling at his waist. His face was grim as always, and he didn't look happy. She knew it was about the Egg. He had come for a fight.

"What?" she said.

He stopped in front of her, folding his arms. "You should have consulted us."

"Maybe," she agreed. "And what would you have said?"

"That we need the Egg."

She met his eyes. "That's the problem. Everybody wanted the Egg to win, and I get it. Its power could have given us an edge. But the Egg was never really ours to use. It belongs to the Flames. It belongs with them in Arncrag. And we don't have the right to just take it for ourselves. Besides, the Egg's power is beyond human comprehension, and that makes it is too dangerous for us to weaponize."

"But we would have been careful! We only would have used it on Francis—"

"You want blood, Nathaniel. That's all you want."

"And you don't?" he asked.

"I want justice. But I also want peace."

"So do I," he said defensively.

"Are you sure?"

Nathaniel scowled and turned away, shoving his hands into his pockets. For the first time, he actually looked his age. "I want to be a Rider, Dree. Like you. And yes, I want vengeance on Francis."

"And you think that will help you what . . . be a better Rider? Become a man?"

He turned back to her. "It's so easy to be noble when you have no one to avenge. When your whole family is still right here with you."

Dree was taken aback. "Excuse me?"

"Your parents are alive. Your siblings. My father died when I was an infant. My mother raised me alone among dragons. She taught me how to be a Rider, how to be true and just and noble. And do you know what she got for that?"

Dree didn't answer.

"Death," he said coolly. "Her dragon was murdered, and so was she. She was betrayed. And so you will excuse me if I don't have mercy for her killers. If I don't think everyone in this world is worth saving. If the Riders are going to rise again, they must be severe as well as just. If my mother had been a little more suspicious, if the Riders had attacked first and destroyed Francis and George, they would be alive."

Dree suddenly felt a pang of sympathy for Nathaniel. She could hear the anger and hurt in his voice.

She slid off the hybrid, facing him. "And what would your mother tell you, if she was here?"

Nathaniel seemed taken aback. Then he scowled and shook his head. "She would tell me that if we become our enemies, then we have already lost the war. It was her favorite saying, actually."

"She sounds like a smart woman. I know we have to win this war, Nathaniel. But we have to win it the right way."

He held her gaze for a moment. "Maybe you Furies aren't so bad after all," he muttered.

"Wait until you see me angry," she replied, smirking. "How is Emmett doing?"

Nathaniel turned grim again. "As far as we can tell, he will never fly again. He is inconsolable."

Dree put a hand on Nathaniel's shoulder. "That wasn't your fault, you know. Emmett wanted to go."

"He was my responsibility," Nathaniel snapped.

"All of that guilt will weigh you down, Nathaniel. It will slow your reflexes and dull your mind. It will rob you of sleep and peace. Sometimes the only way is to let it all go."

She met his eyes.

"We have all lost family. I lost my brother because I didn't have control. That will never happen again."

Nathaniel nodded and walked out of the chamber, leaving Dree to consider everything she had just said. If she truly believed her own words, then she had to stop letting guilt and fear consume her too. Marcus and her father were a part of this war, like she was, and she couldn't control them. In the end, she could only push forward, and do what was right. For the moment, that meant doing everything she could to win the war.

Dree scooped up her torch and got back to work.

Chapter 19

Marcus and Abelard ran through the meadow, moving in silence. Shouts had gone up across the city now, and they could see soldiers making their way toward the burning tavern. It was still aflame, shooting tongues of fire up toward the sky. Marcus looked back, feeling his cheeks burn with shame.

He could have killed someone. He had let his temper get the best of him yet again.

He was no better than Francis.

As the two of them moved into the shadow of the mountains, Abelard slowed, obviously laboring. Marcus could see the slight hunch in his still-injured back, and though he remained stoic, Abelard was obviously in great pain. Marcus wondered how much the man had to fight just to get up and move every morning. And now he had just trekked through the entire mountain range. It only added to Marcus's guilt.

"What are you doing here?" Marcus asked, stepping beside the older man.

The grass rose almost to their waists, like they were wading through a black, still ocean. The sky was clear tonight and the moon cast an eerie white glow over the valley.

Abelard glanced at him. "I heard about what happened with the Egg. Dree came to me after."

"Ah."

Abelard kept his eyes fixed ahead as they walked into the brush, trying to hide his obvious discomfort. "At first I was angry. She should have told you . . . and me. But would you have let her go?"

Marcus paused. "I didn't want her to . . . no."

"Me either. I was angry with her. I thought she gave away our best chance to win the war."

Marcus looked at him, frowning. "She did."

"Maybe," he said calmly. "But she did what she thought was right. I understand now why she did it. And I think she hoped you would understand too. But then you were angry, and things got out of hand . . . she was wrong to say you don't belong here. She was frustrated and sad and tired. She came to find me, and she was in tears. She doesn't cry much, my Dree. She was terribly upset. She wanted to chase after you herself, but I told her I would do it. You two needed time apart to reflect on everything."

"And what about the Egg? How are we supposed to fight without it? How could she give up our one chance at winning?"

Abelard sighed deeply. "You *do* belong here, Marcus. You have Rider blood. Fury blood, no less. But you weren't raised here. You don't know our history. The story of the humans and dragons in Dracone is . . . complicated."

He stopped walking and turned to Marcus. The grass rippled around them.

"Before Francis, dragons and humans were equals. Brothers and sisters. Riders did not partner with a dragon like a soldier and his horse, but rather as siblings. We respected each other. We were friends."

Marcus heard the pain in his voice. "What happened to your dragon, Abelard?"

"I didn't listen to Francis at first," he said softly. "When he began outlawing dragons from Dracone—including those of the Riders—I was outraged. I flouted the law openly, riding Oron over the city daily. He was a wise dragon—a Nightwing, about the size of Lourdvang. But he had old eyes—purple as an amethyst. And he was patient. He knew the humans were changing—that they were afraid of the wild dragon attacks, and that they wanted progress. He told me often that we could not fight the tide.

"They arrested my parents first, and then threatened to take my children too—including Dree. I stopped meeting Oron publicly, to protect my family. Oron returned to Forost, and I saw him only briefly. Sometimes we would fly far from the city, in the south lands, and then I would be happy again for a little while at least. But one week I went to meet him at our usual place on the east range. He was not there."

"What happened to him?" Marcus asked softly.

"He had been sleeping when they found him. He often slept on the mountains, in the open air under the sun. The dragon hunters fell on him from all sides. They murdered him right where he slept."

Abelard shook his head. Marcus could see that the guilt still hung on him.

"The next I saw him . . . his teeth were in a stand. His scales. His heart. They sold him piece by piece." His voice cracked, and he roughly wiped his eyes. "I went mad. I destroyed most of the dragon stands, and then spent some time in a prison. When they released me, I formed the Resistance and protested Francis constantly. It was a few months later at the dock where my back broke, and the long shadow fell on me."

He turned to Marcus and put his hand on his shoulder.

"I lost a brother that day. And Dree knows that. She remembers the old ways. The Egg is dragon magic . . . it was never meant to be in human hands. We didn't have a right to use it, and she realized that. By bringing the Egg back, she could show some respect to the Flames—to the dragons we scorned. I think that was important to her. And for that, I cannot be mad. We have stolen too much from them, and given so little."

Marcus sighed. "Now I just feel like an idiot."

Abelard laughed. "She does it to me too. But she was wrong to say those hurtful things to you, and she will be the first to tell you when we get back, I am sure. You two need to make up. You are our best hope now."

Marcus nodded, and the two of them set off through the valley again, starting the long trek back to Forost. As they walked, Marcus glanced at Abelard, and finally saw him as the leader he really was—not just as a strong man, but as a wise one as well.

"Do you think we still have a chance?" Marcus asked.

"With Dree, there is always a chance. She is far too stubborn to lose." Abelard looked at Marcus. "I am worried for her. And for you. You are Furies, and that is a rare thing. You must learn to control the fire within you."

Marcus paused. "I almost killed people back there."

"Yes. But that was because you lost control. With time, and patience, you will learn. Yes, Dareon almost destroyed the Dragon Riders. But before him were other Furies: Eldred, Kendrin, and Dara the End-Bringer. Heroes that saved Dracone. You have a choice . . . both of you. You will have to harness your power and lead the Riders."

"What about you?"

"I'm old. My time will pass. The future is with you two . . . to win this war, or to lose it."

Marcus looked at him, and then turned back to the mountains.

"We'll be ready."

Chapter 20

Dree moved the welding torch slowly down the seam, immersing herself fully in the shower of red-hot sparks that would have burned anyone else on contact. The sparks covered her bare arms and cheeks and hair without even leaving a mark, sitting like fireflies until they fizzled out forever. Dree had plunged herself into her work as soon as Nathaniel left, pushing the guilt aside. But her mind did wander while she worked, and she still wanted desperately to apologize to Marcus—especially now that she had realized why she was acting so rashly. It wasn't his fault that she was trying to push him away.

For so long, Dree had fended for herself. She had already experienced so much loss at such a young age—getting close to anyone seemed like a mistake. She was better off alone, she had decided. Just her and Lourdvang, and Abi at home.

That had been a good idea in theory . . . until Marcus.

She sat back and looked at the hybrid. Without the Egg it would still be a slightly lesser version of the first one, but it would be dangerous regardless. She still planned on riding it into battle herself, though.

Jack was asleep in the corner, completely exhausted. He had wanted to go after Marcus too, but Abelard had convinced him to stay. Reluctantly, he had sat down, and eventually the exhaustion took him.

Dree was tired too, but she wouldn't sleep until she knew Marcus was okay.

She returned to her work, welding the last section of the leg. The face was lying on the ground a short way ahead—slightly different from Baby Hybrid's. She had again fashioned four long teeth and hollow eyes; but the snout was shorter and broader, while the expression was designed to be fiercer, like a snarling predator hunting its next meal. Her mother said the whole hybrid was likely to give her nightmares, but Dree didn't mind that idea. She hoped it would do the same for Francis when he saw it.

As she worked, she caught a flicker of motion in the corner of her eye. She shut off the torch and turned around to see Marcus slowly walk in the room, looking at his feet. Dree threw down her equipment and rushed forward to meet him. She was about to hug him but stopped short, not wanting to overstep.

"I'm sorry," they both said at the same time.

Dree frowned. "Why are you sorry?"

"Because I should have trusted you to do the right thing. Abelard told me about the dragons . . . about the history, and why you did what you did. I understand now that we never had a right to the dragons' magic. You were just respecting that. And I think maybe you were right to return the Egg. I just really wanted to beat Francis, you know?"

Dree smiled and wrapped him in a hug, catching him completely off guard. Then she felt her cheeks flush and quickly backed away again, tucking her hands into her pockets. "Thank you, Marcus. It wasn't easy, trust me. I want to destroy Francis too, but there has to be a better way. I couldn't live with myself if something as powerful as the Egg got into the wrong hands. Still, I should be saying sorry to you. I didn't mean what I said. *Of course* you belong here. Dracone is your home."

She reached out and took his hand.

Marcus smiled. "I'm not going anywhere, I promise."

Dree let go of his hand and made her way toward the hybrid. "So, she's just about done."

Marcus walked around their creation, surveying every detail. He stopped beside her, nodding.

"You did a great job," he said. "But I'm so worried that it's not enough, Dree."

Dree sighed. She had the same concerns, but she hadn't voiced them until now. "I'm worried too."

Marcus slumped, as if he was hoping she would have some better news. "So what do we do?"

"I don't know," she said, turning back to the hybrid. "I really don't know."

"We're going into a battle we can't possibly win. They outnumber us two to one. We'll all be cut to shreds. I just don't see how we can win, Dree."

A voice suddenly boomed across the chamber as Lourdvang strode inside.

"We will win because we have to," Lourdvang said, stopping and rising up to his full height, his enormous ebony head close to the stalactites. "We needed the Egg to win before, that was true. But when we left for Earth, we barely had any allies—it was just us and some Nightwings. But look at how much has changed since then. All of the Nightwings and Sages are with us, and I believe Nolong even has some Outliers joining the attack. Not to mention all of the Resistance fighters, more of whom seem to join our ranks almost every day. Before, we were just a handful of rebels trying to come up with a plan. Now we're an *army*.

"Don't get me wrong. The fight will be difficult. We will need to work as a team, and our plan will have to be seamless. But I know we can win, together."

"Do you really think we have an army big enough to take on all of those drones?" Dree asked.

Lourdvang stared at her. "There can be no more division. Not between you two, and not between anyone else. If we don't work together, this attack is doomed. And somebody needs to show them that. They need to bring them together. You two need to become true leaders."

Marcus nodded. "He's right. So what's next?"

Dree turned toward the main caves. "We get the others together. It's time to come up with a new plan."

"Wait," Marcus said, taking her arm. "Come with me."

He led her to an empty cavern. She looked around, frowning.

"What's wrong?"

"I did something tonight," Marcus said, looking away. His voice was nearly at a whisper. "I burned down a tavern. I . . . I could have killed people."

"Did you?"

"No, but it was close. The anger . . . it just takes over. I can't control it, Dree. The power that we have. I know you can't control it either. And we don't have a teacher. But maybe you and I could work on it?"

"How?" she asked, looking at her hands.

He shrugged. "Let's start by seeing what we can do."

Dree and Marcus sat face-to-face, cross-legged on the cavern floor. Both of them had their hands up in the air, palms out, and Dree watched curiously as fire lapped off his splayed fingers, small yet constant.

"How are you doing it?" she asked.

Marcus opened his eyes. "Trying to focus the anger, I guess, but not let it take control at the same time. I'm putting the emotions into the flames, and not letting them run through the rest of my body."

Dree frowned and closed her eyes, trying to focus on the fire. It was a strange sensation. She could feel the heat moving through her, like molten lava beneath a volcano, filtering through her veins. She thought of the war, and of Francis, and of her childhood home lying in ruins. The anger simmered, and the fire moved outward, swallowing her heart. She tried to rein the fire in, but felt it pulsating now, threatening to erupt at any time. She opened her eyes and saw that her arms were starting to come ablaze.

"Try to focus it," Marcus said encouragingly, the flames still confined to his fingers.

The fire continued to spread, and Dree tried to bring it back to her hands—to *focus* the anger.

"I can't," she groaned. "It's too much."

"We have to," Marcus said calmly. "We don't want to hurt anyone else by accident."

Dree thought of her little brother. Marcus was right. She kept her hands wide open, not wanting to create a fist and let the fire come racing out. And then something very strange happened.

Fire did escape her hands, but it did not erupt outward. It crossed between her and Marcus and joined his hands—a bridge of fire. Marcus stared at her in amazement as the link between them grew.

Dree felt a sudden sense of calm filter over her, and she met his eyes.

For a moment she felt completely connected. She could feel his fear and guilt and anger. She felt a new focus and a far greater control. Dree held Marcus's gaze as the two slowly let out all of their pent-up emotion. They shared the burden.

"I . . . feel your anger," Marcus said, never breaking eye contact. "And your fears. And more."

"Me too. I . . . it makes it easier to feel it. To know you feel the same." A sudden thought came to her. "Do you remember what Eria said back in the war room? There have never been two Furies at once."

"They always were alone," Marcus agreed. "But we don't have to be."

Dree smiled, letting the fire recede back into her hands. She felt calmer now and in control.

"Should we see what we can do now?" she asked.

He grinned. "Definitely."

They both stood up and faced the wall. Dree felt the calmness flood over her, but it did not suppress the fire. The anger was simply *detached* from her. She clenched her fists, allowing it to swell over her fingers, and then she thrust her hand toward the wall. An orange fireball burst out and struck the rock, exploding into a shower of flame. Marcus followed suit. They unleashed them again and again until they were comfortable aiming at specific targets. The whole chamber was ablaze as they practiced.

Finally, Dree turned to Marcus. "Let's try to spar. We might need to fight hand-to-hand."

Marcus looked at her, hesitant. "Are you going to beat me up?"

"Probably."

She raised her hands, and he followed suit, both allowing a bit of fire to flicker on their fists. She stepped in with a light punch and he parried her, stepping quickly back. He had just allowed himself a self-satisfied grin when she grabbed his arm and twisted it forward, forcing him to the ground.

"Ow," he said.

She laughed and let him up. "Don't let your guard down."

They sparred for another hour, and Dree beat him every time. But Marcus was getting better—a little more familiar with how to block and avoid her armlocks, at the very least. Near the end he almost managed to knock her down before she pinned him again, laughing.

"Not bad," she said.

"My entire body hurts," he replied with a laugh.

She climbed off him and pulled him to his feet. "Ready to give a speech?"

"I hate speeches," he said.

"Me too. But I think it's time. If we're going to be Furies, we had better lead the way. Together."

Marcus smiled. "Together." He paused. "You can do the talking, though."

Dree rolled her eyes and started for the tunnel. If they had to give a speech, then so be it. But they were going to need allies if they had any chance of convincing the group. And she had someone in mind.

Chapter 21

Dree and Marcus found Nathaniel sitting alone in the war room, his blue eyes locked on the wall. Dree wondered if he was still thinking about their conversation. She hoped so. They needed him to be ready.

"We need to talk," Dree said, stopping in front of him.

Nathaniel looked up. "Well, if it isn't the noble Rider and her boyfriend."

Dree stiffened, and Marcus put a hand on her arm. "Calm," he reminded her.

Dree sighed. "Right. Nathaniel, the hybrid is ready. Marcus and I want to lead the attack, but we need some support in there. I can count on my dad, I think, but we would like your support too."

Nathaniel stood up—he was taller than both of them, and he looked down, raising his eyebrows.

"You've already given away our most powerful weapon, and now you want to *lead* everyone?"

Dree didn't back down. "Yes. The Egg is gone, as it should be. We had no right to its dragon magic. Now it's time to move forward. Together."

"Like how the decision to give away the Egg was made together?"

"I was wrong to go off on my own. I should have at least made my case to you all—I should have trusted that you would do what was right. I won't betray you again, I promise. But I need you to help me."

Nathaniel started to pace. "Listen, I know why you did it. And you made some fair points about our strategy. I might have been a bit too . . . eager. But I also don't know if we have the strength to win anymore, regardless. In fact, I know we don't. Forty war-worthy dragons perhaps, at most. Twenty humans. Against who knows how many drones? It is going to be a massacre."

"At this rate, yeah," Marcus said. "But we need to stop arguing. We need to work together."

Nathaniel snorted. "You want to win a war by holding hands? Good luck with that."

"We need to try," Dree said fiercely. "No more talks about whose strategy is better. The Egg is gone, and Teen Hybrid is finished. There is no point in waiting anymore. We need to attack tomorrow, before the drones return.

We have a simple plan, but we think it might stand a chance."

"We're going to call the meeting now," Marcus said. "Will you get your men together?"

Nathaniel turned to them, hesitating. "Fine. But you have some convincing to do."

Dree and Marcus stood nervously at the front of the war room as the last of the Resistance fighters and dragons shuffled into the cavern, forming a large group in front of them. Dree scanned over the faces of the human fighters—some young, some old, and many looking like she felt: tired and worn down, but determined.

Her eyes fell on Ciaran, who stood at the front of the group, a sword sheathed to her belt. Her raven hair was tied into a severe ponytail, revealing the proud lines of her cheeks and chin. Dree wondered if the fiery girl would ever agree to follow her and Marcus, as she was a few years older. She had a lot of influence within the group.

Abelard stood in front of Dree as well, watching her. She could see the curiosity on his face. She straightened and tried to look brave.

"We have called this meeting because there has been some confusion lately . . . some of it caused by me. There have been arguments and debates and harsh words. We have had fighters and dragons acting on their own. Many have presented their own strategies, and there has been even more fighting."

She saw a lot of the fighters glancing at each other, and she knew she had guessed right. Abelard nodded.

"The Egg is gone," Marcus cut in, stepping up beside her. "It has been returned to the red dragons."

There was angry murmuring around the room, and Ciaran stepped forward, frowning. Dree noticed that her slender hand had almost subconsciously fallen on the pommel of her silver longsword.

"Why was this done without consulting us? *You* were the ones who said that the Egg was our best chance," she said angrily.

Dree nodded. "Because I did not trust everyone to make the right choice and return the Egg to the Flames. And that was wrong."

Marcus held up his hands to stop any rebuttals. "It doesn't matter anymore. It's gone, and we have to discuss what to do next."

The low ripple of conversation became louder. Dree could feel the anger growing. She and Marcus were losing control.

"The Egg was never ours," she said firmly. "And it should never have been taken in the first place. Many died because of that mistake. But the point is that there is no more need to wait. Every day the drones attack us, digging ever deeper into the mountainside. The time to act is now. I vote that we attack tomorrow with our full strength. We have a simple plan, but I believe it is the right one. A joint aerial and ground attack, with our *full* force. The dragons and their riders—led by Teen Hybrid—will head directly for the palace, while a ground team disables the surface-to-air weapons. Teen Hybrid will engage Baby Hybrid, and the main force of dragons and riders will draw out the drones and engage. Our advantage is close combat—we want to stay on them and prevent sweeping runs or missiles. When an opening is made, a small team will head straight for the control room. If we get to the room, we may be able to deactivate the drone arm. Francis will likely be in the room, directing the battle, so we can arrest him as well."

"Now we're supposed to follow these children?" one fighter scoffed. "Ridiculous."

Lourdvang growled and stalked up beside Dree, causing a few fighters to quickly step back again. "These two 'children' have done more for this war than anyone in the room. They deserve your trust."

"That's fine and well," another woman said, "coming from her dragon."

"*Her* dragon?" Lourdvang snarled, meeting the woman's gaze. "We are not pets."

The woman took a step back. "I didn't mean that, and you know it."

"Easy," Dree said, resting her hand on Lourdvang's leg. "All of this infighting helps no one."

She stepped forward, looking out over the assembled group.

"Francis Xidorne kills more people every day. More dragons, more humans. Every day people starve in the ruins of their former homes. We didn't ask for this war. Xidorne is power hungry, and the people in this room are the last defense against him. Some of you represent the last of the Dragon Riders—and your responsibility is clear: to protect those who cannot protect themselves, and to uphold justice and peace. The dragons are in danger of being wiped out, and so are we. So is our way of life. All of you have chosen to stop this. You have chosen to risk your lives to defend Dracone. That makes us brothers and sisters, and we have to work together. We have to believe that we can win, or we don't stand a chance. I know Marcus and I are young, but we know what we're doing. Marcus knows the drones better than anyone in this room, and we have both been in the palace and faced Francis before. Please trust that we can lead you."

The war room fell into silence, and Dree stood there, proud. She had felt the flames building in her as she spoke, and she knew that her eyes might have been flashing with very real fire, but she contained herself.

"She's right," a loud voice said.

Dree looked up and was shocked to see Nathaniel step forward, his face grim.

"We need to attack," he continued solemnly, "and I can think of no two people better prepared to lead us." He stopped in front of Dree and Marcus, nodding. "I will follow you into battle tomorrow, Furies."

"As will I," Abelard said, smiling at Dree. "It is time to end this war."

To Dree's surprise, Ciaran nodded from the front row, as did Eria, and slowly the rest followed. The dragons at the back roared their approval as well, sending black smoke shooting across the room.

"We leave first thing in the morning," Dree said. "Go get some rest. We'll review the plan before leaving at first light."

As the Resistance began filing out, Dree turned to Nathaniel and nodded. "Thank you," she said.

Nathaniel smiled. "What can I say? You convinced me. You were right about the Riders. My mother always told me the same thing. We can't hide from it any longer—it's time to face our destiny."

Chapter 22

Marcus turned to the others, feeling very uncomfortable. "How do I look?"

Dree covered her mouth. "Great!" she said, trying to suppress a laugh.

Marcus scowled and looked down at himself. He had donned some traditional Dragon Rider armor and a long sword that hung in a bejeweled leather scabbard at his waist, dangling almost to the floor. The armor was raven black and crimson, with a helmet with two curving, winged armored plates that stretched down to his chin. It had heavy iron gauntlets and a solid chest plate that had Marcus teetering forward with every step. All of it felt unnaturally heavy and ungainly. He took off the helmet, shaking his head.

"I'll go without."

Dree shook her head. "You need the protection."

"But there are other people who need this more," he said firmly. "I can ride the dragons without armor."

Dree picked up her own sword and swung it back and forth gracefully, the blade moving smoothly through the air like she was painting a picture. Marcus felt a surge of jealousy. Dree looked like a Dragon Rider, even though she had opted out of the armor as well. Her leather jerkin exposed her corded, muscular arms, and she held the sword like it was a natural extension of her hand. Behind her, Nathaniel had donned his armor as well; his helmet shone like a flame, and he had both a sword and a bow strapped to his back. He too looked like a Rider—strong and tall and handsome. Marcus felt like a child.

He turned away, not wanting to practice with the sword in front of them. He just had to hope it wouldn't come to an actual swordfight—he knew he wouldn't last very long if it did. He had managed to survive the last attack on the palace, but only barely. Marcus watched Dree from the corner of his eye as she danced across the cavern, weighing the different swords to find one with the right heft. She had forged swords and shields for years and was an expert in honing their balance. Some of these weapons had been stolen by Resistance fighters from Wilhelm's Forge, and it was even possible she herself had made them.

They were soon interrupted by the whirring of motors, and Marcus turned to see Teen Hybrid sail into the armory,

Jack perched atop it with a satisfied grin. The new hybrid was a bit smaller than the first but was also a sleeker design, with short, angled wings and legs that tucked into its body. Flames still shone in its black iron eyes, and the dual machine guns remained fixed ominously beneath the wings. There were two missiles as well—they were vital to the plan. But no one had actually flown the hybrid yet—they were supposed to be doing the last few tests. Obviously, Jack had decided it was time to try.

Teen Hybrid floated to the ground, its iron legs unfurling to catch itself on the cavern floor. Jack hopped off.

"You already tested it?" Dree asked in amazement.

Jack nodded, grinning. He looked like a child who had just gotten a brand-new toy. "I knew you kids were busy, so I took the liberty. She flies great." He walked around the hybrid, pointing out some changes he had made, and Dree and Marcus looked at each other incredulously. Jack had been busy. "I added a whole lot of bells and whistles in the last couple of days," he said proudly, pointing to something beneath the chamber. "Check this out: a power amplifier. Something I was working on back at the beginning of all this but never quite managed to figure out. Well, things seem a little different in Dracone. It will only last for a minute or so, but you can now amp up the power so that this baby has increased speed and firing rate. Also, the machine guns will now alternate *or* fire simultaneously, and I added these."

He pointed to a few small nozzles on the wings.

"Tiny accelerators I fabricated out of the leftovers. It will give us more maneuverability . . . barrel rolls, faster dives and turns, you name it. She'll move as fast as any drone now . . . I promise you that."

"This is amazing," Marcus said, shaking his head. "You actually improved our design."

Jack shrugged. "Figured it was the least I can do, since I helped create those cursed drones in the first place. It felt pretty cathartic, actually." He turned to Dree. "I would like to fly her into battle."

Dree and Marcus looked at each other. "You're not exactly used to flying—" Dree started.

"I've piloted a plane or two in my time," he said. "This has become my war. I saw what those drones have done. I want to help, and my place is on Teen Hybrid. You can ride Lourdvang."

Dree nodded. "He would like that, I suppose. What about you, Marcus?"

"I'll ask Erdath or Nolong," he said. "You're sure, Uncle Jack?"

"I'm sure." He folded his arms and turned to Marcus. "Now, not to sound like an uncle, but you two should probably eat something and get to bed. We kind of have a big day tomorrow."

The fire flickered in the middle of the cavern, and the group cast shadows against the walls like ghostly apparitions. A spit hung over the fire, where a pheasant and some corn cooked over the open flame. Marcus, Dree, Abelard, Nathaniel, Jack, and Lourdvang were gathered there, all of them lost in their thoughts.

Marcus was eating half a pheasant, and the grease was dripping down his chin as he bit into the succulent wing meat. He hadn't really stopped to eat a full meal since they'd been back to Dracone, and it was absolutely delicious. Dree had already devoured a whole pheasant across from him. Now she was leaning back and staring at the fire. He saw the flames in her dark eyes.

He thought of all the Riders throughout history who had sat here in Forost, eating a meal just like this. He wondered if his mother had been here often. If she too had sat here and eaten roasted pheasant.

"What was it like?" Marcus asked Abelard. "When the Dragon Riders protected the realm?"

Abelard smiled, the light playing tricks on his grizzled face. "I suppose I was the only one here to remember it, wasn't I?" He glanced at Marcus. "A king ruled then, as I'm sure you've heard. He was a good man . . . King Loron the Second. The Childless King, they called him. Riders had already protected the realm for centuries, and it was no different then. There were fifty Riders left before the purge. Our main headquarters were here, in Forost, though Riders and their dragons could go anywhere undisturbed. A council of five elder Dragon Riders and dragons helped lead us, though one often held the most power. We kept the wild dragons at bay, halted invaders from the south, and maintained peace.

All we had to do was fly over a disturbance in the city—a fight, a crime, an angry mob—and the perpetrators would flee. None dared offend a Rider. We could keep the peace without ever shedding any blood."

He spoke softly, his eyes back on the fire now.

"But our lives were not only spent as guardians. Most Riders were from ancient and wealthy families—wealth they had accumulated over many years, as naturally they were often the first to find gold and diamonds and other treasures, being explorers. Many grew jealous. I see it now—our folly in separating ourselves from the people. It was supposed to be our mandate to use the wealth to help others—to build homes and feed the poor and help expand the city. Many did, including my family."

Marcus frowned. "What happened? Why did everyone turn on you if that was the case?"

Abelard sighed deeply. "There were other families who grew proud. They worried more about their own fortunes than the people. They built huge mansions in the country and flaunted their gold and jewelry. Many grew vain and forgot their duties. When King Loron died, there was a fight over who would be the successor. That is when Francis Xidorne rose to power. He preached the need for a council and a true democracy—an end to our age-old monarchy. He was probably right in that regard, and he soon swept to power with ease—it was more a revolution than a vote, though.

"A few accidents befell some of the likely heirs to the throne—I suspect through Francis's doing. The path had been cleared for him. Francis did a few things that were very wise: He appealed to people's fear of the wild dragons, he appealed to everyone's desire to be wealthy, and he turned both of those emotions against us—the symbols of ancient wealth and assumed power. He sold the people on a new world of technology and expansion, where normal people could become wealthy. He said the dragons were a scourge. Everything changed almost overnight. He consolidated his power and banned the Riders and started the hunt of the dragons. He removed key members of the dragon families and seized their homes. He erased the old world and replaced it with the new."

"And he did it with the blood of dragons," Lourdvang said sadly.

"Yes," Abelard agreed. "And now with the blood of everyone who doesn't fit into his vision of a new Dracone."

Marcus hesitated. "So, say we do beat him . . . what will happen after? There are no more kings."

"No," Abelard said. "We must continue with a democracy. It is fine if the Dragon Riders no longer have the wealth and privilege of yore. But with Francis gone, we will still be able to help protect this realm and maintain the peace. We can oversee the new elections and find a better leader."

Nathaniel nodded. "We have to rebuild the Riders as well. That means finding the descendants of the old Riders and training them to ensure the legacy continues. And now perhaps . . . to help restore the dragons to their former numbers."

"That will take time," Lourdvang said gruffly. "We have lost almost three-quarters of our population since the war began." His great blue eyes narrowed, reflecting the campfire. "Francis will pay for that."

"First we have to beat the drones," Jack said grimly. "Everything else can wait."

"Yes," Abelard said. "And on that note, we had better get some sleep."

Everyone rose to their feet, and Marcus started for his little makeshift cot of crumpled clothes. He felt someone grab his arm, and turned to see Jack ushering him to the side. Marcus followed him, frowning.

"What's wrong?" Marcus asked.

"Oh . . . no . . . nothing is wrong," Jack said, shifting uncomfortably.

Jack's cheeks were a little flushed, and he stuffed his hands in his pockets.

"What is it, then?" Marcus asked.

"I just want to let you know that I really am proud of you. Whatever happens tomorrow, I always have been proud, even if I never said it. I know . . . well, I wasn't really a great father figure. Never had much practice, you know. You deserved someone to take you to school in the mornings and help with homework and cook dinner and all that stuff . . .

you had to do it all by yourself since you were just a little kid. And you never complained once . . . in fact, you grew into the young man I see now. I'm sorry, Marcus. I guess I just wasn't ready to be a father, and I should have done more."

Marcus shook his head. "You were a role model for me, Uncle Jack. Maybe you didn't always cook dinner or go to my parent–teacher meetings, but you taught me about robotics and programming and things that I loved. You think most kids got that? I know it probably wasn't easy on you when my dad took off. But you never complained to me either. And I know I wasn't exactly the easiest kid to raise . . ."

Jack snorted. "Why? Because you were chasing thunderstorms and building robots?"

Marcus laughed. "Both. But I wouldn't change anything. Thank you."

Jack fixed his glasses uncomfortably, and for the first time in Marcus's life, he reached over and gave him a hug. Then he stepped away again, scratching his neck. "Well . . . uh . . . time for bed, I think."

"Yeah," Marcus said, shifting. "We'll see you in the morning."

Jack hurried off to his corner, and Marcus went and lay down on the makeshift cot.

"You two are so awkward," Dree said. "But kind of cute."

"Thanks," Marcus muttered.

"Get some sleep. Try not to think about the massive battle we have to fight tomorrow."

Marcus sighed. "Yeah. I'll do my best."

There was a long moment of silence, and then Dree turned to him.

"Whatever happens tomorrow, I'm glad you showed up in that storm, Marcus Brimley."

He smiled in the darkness. "So am I. We're going to win, Dree. We have to."

She rolled back, staring up at the distant stalactites. "You sound like a Rider."

"I hope so," he said. "I'm not sure that I feel like one yet."

"You will," she whispered. "You were born to be one."

Dree lifted her hands, and they flickered with a radiant red-and-blue flame.

"Stay close to me tomorrow. Let's find out what two Furies can do."

Chapter 23

D ree woke to the sound of footsteps, and she rolled over sleepily to see fighters and dragons already moving about outside of their chamber. Despite her brave words, a sick, nervous feeling settled into Dree's stomach almost immediately. She tasted acrid bile in her mouth, and her tongue felt as coarse as sandpaper. Marcus blinked awake beside her, and by the stark whiteness that immediately spread over his face, she knew he was thinking the same thing. It was the morning of the battle.

A true battle, the kind that not everyone came back from—in this case, maybe not any of them.

They both put their jackets on and strapped their swords to their hips in silence, neither finding reason to have a conversation. Lourdvang rose and stretched in the far corner, his eyes on Dree, and she saw Jack get up and start inspecting Teen Hybrid, readying her for battle. The silence in the cavern was heavy—broken only by the footsteps and quiet voices echoing through the tunnels. Everyone was preparing.

"So this is what war feels like," Marcus said quietly. "Before, we were always sneaking around, or getting caught unaware and just getting thrown into it. This is the first time we've gone into a full battle knowingly—no sneaking around this time. A real battle where two sides meet full on. Now I get it, I think. It's not what I thought. War is a sick feeling in your stomach and shaking hands and wishing that you were anywhere else in the world."

Dree nodded. "Not exactly what they sing songs about, is it?"

"No." Marcus stopped and looked at her. "Are you afraid?"

"Very. You?"

"Terrified."

Dree smiled and took his hand. "Listen . . . about what I said during our fight—"

"It's in the past, Dree. You already apologized."

She shook her head. "I know. But I just want you to know that you belong here as much as anyone I have ever met. And I am proud to be defending *our* home together."

Marcus smiled. "So am I."

Dree squeezed his hand. "We'd better go join the others."

The four of them hurried to the war room. From there, the Resistance army would leave through an opening on the side of the mountain and make their journey to the city. Forost was lit only by torches, as ever, but Dree knew that it was morning outside. There would be no more stealthy raids. They were going to attack in the light of day.

Dragons, Resistance fighters, and displaced families were milling about everywhere, preparing for the departure. Dree saw her family waiting with Abelard and hurried over. Abi wrapped her in a hug.

"I don't want you to go," she said, tears streaming down her face.

Dree met her eyes. "I have to, so that we can go home again. You keep an eye on the boys."

Her two little brothers were holding on to her mother's legs, for once completely silent. Dree suspected that even they could feel the tension in the air. Some people were crying, and many were saying their goodbyes, wrapped in the kind of embraces that surface only when you know you may not come home. Nathaniel stood alone, his eyes on the floor. She wondered if he was thinking about poor Emmett.

"See you soon, boys," Dree said gently, and her brothers hurried over and gave her a hug.

When she stood up, her mother took her shoulders, fighting back tears. "You be careful, Driele, do you hear me? No doing anything stupid out there. Just take out that awful man and get back here safe."

Dree smiled. "I will, Mom. I can do this."

Her mother hugged her, the tears spilling out now. "When did you go and become a woman?"

"I don't know. But I had a good role model," Dree said.

Her mother sniffled, hugging her tighter. "I'm proud of you. Take care of your father."

"He'll be fine too," Abelard said gruffly, scooping up one of the boys and tousling his hair. "He may be an old man, but he's still got a little fight left in him. Right?" he said, tickling Otto.

Abelard looked at the family. He wore full dragon armor, crimson and black, and a great sword hung at his side. A beard had crept down his neck and past his cheeks, but he still looked much younger than the ghost of a man Dree had lived with for so many years.

He was to ride Erdath into battle—the two leaders riding as one.

"We'll be back for dinner," Abe said. "And tonight we will eat in Dracone. Maybe in the palace?"

"Really?" Abi asked, wiping her eyes with her sleeve.

He winked. "Maybe so."

He put Otto down and gave Dree's mother a kiss. It was the first time Dree had seen them kiss since she was a child. They had been so distant for so long, but it seemed that all of those difficult years were now forgotten.

"Remember, you're not twenty anymore," her mother said sternly, wagging a finger at Abelard.

He laughed. "Don't I know it. Come on, Dree. The sun is rising."

The group of fighters started down the tunnel toward the hidden opening, and the families stayed behind to wave them off. Dree waved goodbye to her sister one last time, wondering if she would ever see her again.

Don't think like that, she scolded herself. She had to focus on the battle.

Before she did, though, she grabbed her father's hand.

"What is it?" he asked.

"Be safe out there, Dad. I feel like I just got you back, and I don't want to lose you again."

Abelard pulled her into a hug, a strong hand resting on the back of her head.

"My Driele," he said, his voice muffled in her hair. "I'm so sorry I drifted away all those years. You are much better than your father. A true Rider, I do not doubt it. And I want to be old and gray to see you become what you were born to be. I won't leave you. And don't you go do anything stupid either, brave as you are."

Dree choked out a laugh. "I won't."

He released her and met her eyes. "I am so proud of you, Dree."

He walked toward the rest of the fighters, shouting orders, while Dree climbed up onto Lourdvang's back and Jack settled atop Teen Hybrid. The other Riders mounted their own dragons, careful not to touch scales with exposed skin. All wore the fire-resistant armor except, of course, for Dree and Marcus. Marcus was mounted on Nolong—who had proudly agreed to partner with him for the battle—and Abelard soon climbed aboard the great black hulk of Erdath.

Abelard turned back to the group.

"Make no mistake, this attack is risky. There are many drones, and many soldiers, and the odds are against us. But today, we are Dragon Riders. Today we take back the city and overthrow Xidorne. With a new sun comes a new future. Fight hard and know that your cause is a just one. The drones are powerful, yes, and they are a fearsome enemy. But they are machines. We have heart and passion and the knowledge that we cannot lose. Our families, our friends, and our people count on us. And so we ride!"

With that, Erdath burst out into open air, and with a resounding cheer, the rest of the new Dragon Riders followed suit. Marcus and Dree were first, followed by Nathaniel and his new mount, and then the dragons flooded out of the opening and swept upward on the current: fifteen armored Riders and their mounts, and another thirty solo dragons beyond that—black and gold and speckled with some green.

The other fighters—those who didn't have armor—had already left for the city. They would be infiltrating on the ground, trying to take out soldiers and any surface-to-air defenses as well—trebuchets, crossbows, and catapults with nets.

Dree looked to the east as they rode up above the mountain, sailing on the cold wind.

The sun was glowing on the horizon like a torch, turning the clouds pink and chasing the darkness away. Dree sat atop Lourdvang, the wind beating into her hair, and she glanced behind her to see the army floating on the wind. It looked like a dream, or an old memory that had long ago slipped from Dracone.

Marcus flew beside her, Nolong's golden scales catching the sunlight beneath him. To Dree's left was her father, looking just like the man she remembered from her childhood—he sat tall and straight, his hair billowing out behind him, his blue eyes proud. Close behind him was Nathaniel, who wore a grim smile. The rest followed. Not all had come from Rider families, as one could see in the way they flew. Many looked scared and uncomfortable, while the true Riders seemed at home. Ciaran rode without a helmet, her long black hair flapping behind her, as if her shadow was racing to keep pace with her.

The Riders were flanked on either side by the solo dragons—Sages and Nightwings, along with five Outliers who had joined the attack, their emerald-green skin standing out in the sea of black and gold. Dree knew that an army like this hadn't been seen in Dracone for many decades. It was a beautiful sight, but she still wondered if it would be enough. At the very least, she had lived to see the return of the Dragon Riders—if only for a fateful morning, and one last valiant charge.

And then, of course, there was Teen Hybrid, holding up a scared but determined Jack. He gave Dree a curt nod, and she returned it. If their plan was to work, Teen Hybrid was going to need to perform and knock out the original, as well as lead the attack on the palace to open the way for the rest of them. If she malfunctioned, they were all doomed.

"It will all have to happen very fast," Abelard called over the wind. "The drones will respond quickly."

"It will be," Dree shouted back.

Once again, she wondered if she would make it back. She kept thinking about the danger for everyone else, but it was just as likely that she could die in the battle too. It was a strange, uncomfortable thought, but Dree also knew that she would trade her life to rid Dracone of Francis and the drones forever.

As long as they won today, nothing else mattered.

"You be careful up there," Lourdvang said, as if reading her thoughts.

"You too, little brother," she admonished. "Protect those wings."

He snorted, shooting out a puff of black smoke. "We're going to have to try to get close to the Destroyers. Their armor is too strong for my fire. I need to rip them apart."

"I know. If you can get me close enough, Marcus showed me where their control panels are—he said that should be their most vulnerable section. A sword in the right place will put one down."

The army flew over the mountain range with the rising sun, and it was not long until the city rose up before them, perched on the edge of the sparkling lake and surrounded by the vast ring of death and destruction that the drones had wrought: thousands of homes turned into nothing but rubble. From the skies, the full extent could truly be seen—piles of stone and wood lined the road, while starving survivors huddled in the ruins.

Dree's anger rose inside her again, controlled now, and she tightened her grip on Lourdvang and exchanged a look with Marcus. He nodded grimly. As one, they drifted gracefully on the wind, angling toward the white palace that sat in the middle of the city—Francis's seat of power. Dree's eyes widened.

There weren't just ten drones sitting above the palace, as they had guessed.

Francis must have known they were coming.

The entire army had been assembled: Some fifty drones hovered there. Destroyers and Trackers filled the sky like a murder of crows just waiting for battle, their terrible weapons brimming with death.

She heard gasps and cries going up from the other warriors, but she knew they couldn't go back now. The drones would chase them and carve them up. There was only one thing they could do. *Attack.*

Dree raised her sword overhead as Lourdvang angled his wings and swept toward the city.

"For the dragons!" she shouted, her voice carrying over the wind.

"For Dracone!" Abelard said, raising his own sword.

The swarm of dragons straightened into an arrow pha-
lanx as they approached the drones, with Dree, Marcus,
and Abelard at the lead. Lourdvang roared, spewing fire
and smoke, and the other dragons followed suit until the
roar split through the air like thunder. Dree saw people
below running for cover.

Dree felt her anger swirling through her, and she lifted
her free hand off Lourdvang's scales, watching as the crimson fire swirled around her fingers, growing ever larger. Dree
narrowed her eyes.

Then she closed her fist and launched a fireball toward
the waiting drones.

Chapter 24

Marcus watched as Dree's massive fireball streaked across the sky like a meteor bursting through the atmosphere. It must have been ten feet across—neither of them had ever created anything like it.

The fireball slammed into one of the Destroyers, expanding larger still and enveloping the entire drone in flames just as the gathered drone army surged forward to attack. Marcus heard a great cheer go up from the rest of the Riders around, but they were quickly silenced. The armor-plated Destroyer raced right through the fireball, almost completely unscathed. The drones opened fire.

"Watch out!" he screamed to Nolong, as a missile raced right toward them.

Nolong dove sharply, and the missile flew right past Marcus's head, screaming into the main bulk of the attacking dragon army and exploding spectacularly. The thud of machine guns filled the air as the Trackers and Destroyers started shooting, and the dragons responded with a wave of fire—the orange of Nightwings, the autumn colors of Sages, and the acid-green of the Outliers. The multicolored flames spread across the sky like a second dawn, brighter than anything Marcus had ever seen.

"We need to clear the way for Teen Hybrid!" Marcus shouted.

Nolong wheeled upward again, pursuing one of the ponderous Destroyers through the cloud of drones. Its ivory wings were shaking as it unleashed deadly volleys of bullets, tearing through an Outlier's wings. The two sides had merged fully now, and Marcus could see Dree and Lourdvang being chased by two Trackers. The Destroyer ahead of them turned right, and Nolong followed, his eyes locked on his prey.

"You have him," Marcus urged, trying to keep track of the Destroyer in the chaos.

Nolong closed on the Destroyer quickly and locked his great talons on a wing, sending them both into a free-fall. Fighting the violent g-forces, Marcus struggled to hold on. "Pull!" he shouted.

Nolong roared, his entire body rippling with corded muscle, and then he yanked the huge white wing clean off of the Destroyer. The disabled drone plummeted into the palace courtyard and exploded.

Marcus patted his side. "Nice one, Nolong!"

"Many more to go," he rumbled, heading back into the open sky.

He was right. Marcus saw that many of the dragons were taking hits. Three were already down, as was one Rider—an older man named Gonly who had been a farmer in a nearby village. Marcus spotted Nathaniel and his dragon about a hundred feet up, slashing at the drones as they whizzed past, screaming fierce battle cries. Ciaran was not far either, diving with her dragon after another huge Destroyer. They looked like true Riders: one with their dragons. Marcus searched the sky for the most important person: Jack.

He spotted him almost immediately on a headlong course for the palace. The way was clear.

Teen Hybrid suddenly unleashed its two missiles on the palace, collapsing a huge section of the wall to allow ground troops to break inside. Jack then opened fire with the machine guns, taking out many of the crossbows, trebuchets, and other air defenses as planned. They crumbled into shattered wood under the intense fire, and Teen Hybrid swooped over the ruins, heading back for the main battle.

Beyond him, Marcus saw that the control room was still exposed where the ceiling had been blown apart by Baby Hybrid during Marcus and Dree's last trip to the palace—

and Francis Xidorne stood there calmly, watching the battle unfold. He looked smug, confident. A reserve of some ten drones flanked the control room—protecting Francis and waiting for action.

The message was clear: Francis didn't need his walls. He had the drones.

Marcus was just about to dive for Francis when Baby Hybrid entered the battle.

She zoomed in out of nowhere, firing bullets and missiles and downing two dragons almost instantly. Marcus watched in horror as she whirled around for another pass, gunning down the Dragon Rider Eria and her dragon Orlon in a hail of bullets. Both fell limply toward the ground far below. As Marcus had feared, the dragons were no match for Baby Hybrid. Only another hybrid could destroy their work.

On cue, Jack sped past him atop Teen Hybrid, heading straight for the original.

The two hybrids launched into an aerial dance, and Marcus lost sight of them as Nolong dove back into the fray. Concerned for Jack, he caught a glimpse of them again high above, where they were exchanging fire. Teen Hybrid erupted in sparks as the bullets nipped into its wing, and Jack steered it out of the way. As the two hybrids made another pass at each other and turned, Jack used the new accelerators to wheel about more sharply, beating Baby Hybrid to the turn. As the original tried to follow the maneuver, Jack fired everything he had.

Bullets erupted into the hull of the original, slicing through the lighter metal plating and finally connecting with the power cells. When the bullets hit, one of the power cells blew, shattering one side of the hybrid and sending her cartwheeling out of the sky toward the distant ground. He heard his uncle whoop, and the call was taken up by the rest of the fighters below him.

Marcus pumped his fist and turned back to the battle. Maybe they still had a chance after all.

Nolong managed to take down another two Trackers, ripping them apart savagely, but none were as successful as Jack. He was downing drones everywhere with Teen Hybrid. The drones soon caught on. Jack flew past, pursued by five Trackers. And though he was putting Teen Hybrid through every maneuver possible, they were closing in fast. Marcus saw a flash of spark as the first bullets connected with the hybrid's hull, tearing some steel plating clean off the wing.

"We have to help him, Nolong!" Marcus shouted.

Nolong took off after Jack, managing to latch on to one of the chasing Trackers and rip off its wing. The Tracker went spiraling downward, plunging right through the battle and scattering drones and dragons alike.

"Hang on, Jack!" Marcus cried.

His uncle managed to open fire on another Tracker, blasting it apart; but as he turned to avoid the wreckage, one of the drones finally connected with a power cell. Teen Hybrid's right wing burst into flame, and Jack shouted, trying to avoid the blazing fire. He crawled toward the left wing, losing control.

"Jump!" Marcus said.

The fire spread rapidly, heading for the remaining power cells, and Marcus saw Jack give a last command to the hybrid before he leapt off the side. Another power cell blew, and Teen Hybrid flew toward the ground like a flaming arrow—aiming right at one of the massive crossbows that were launching steel arrows into the air. It connected and exploded, taking the weapon out with it. Marcus felt his stomach turn as he watched another hybrid vanish in fire, but it had done its job and then some. It had cracked the palace open, and it had even taken out its predecessor. And now they had to save Uncle Jack.

"Dive!" Marcus said.

Nolong was way ahead of him. He angled his golden wings and they plunged after a flailing Jack, right through the thick of the air battle. Nolong caught the back of Jack's armor with an extended talon and opened his great golden wings just in time to slow their rapid descent. They swept toward the ground, and Nolong gently released Jack onto the cobblestone street. He rolled and then jumped back to his feet.

"Get to cover!" Marcus shouted.

"Be careful!" Jack said, and then hurried toward a brick shop.

Nolong launched himself back into the air, surveying the battle as they climbed.

"We're in trouble, young Rider," he said gravely. "Their numbers are too great."

Marcus saw another dead dragon slam into a building. "Yeah. Let's try to fix that."

Dree plunged her sword into the back of a drone, stabbing right into a power cell. The drone shorted out, and Lourdvang pushed off the back of the Tracker, letting it fall toward the palace. Dree looked around.

They had destroyed many drones already, but the Resistance's numbers were dwindling fast. Many of the solo dragons had been taken out first, having only two eyes instead of four to watch out for danger. But even the Riders were being gunned down now. She counted at least five that had gone down already, and she watched as another dragon and Rider were hit by a missile and vanished. She looked away, sickened.

"We can't win this way," Lourdvang said.

"I know."

She had already watched Teen Hybrid get blown out of the sky. Even though it had done its job, they had now lost their most potent weapon. Erdath and Abelard swept past, pursued by drones. Behind them, Ciaran was fighting madly, already bleeding from a severe bullet wound on her shoulder.

"Help her!" Dree said.

Lourdvang turned toward Ciaran, and Dree ducked as a Tracker nearly took off her head. The storm of bullets was everywhere, bouncing off dragons' scales or ripping through vulnerable wings. Lourdvang already had two holes on his left wing—thankfully small enough that he could still fly.

They slammed into one of the drones chasing Ciaran, and Lourdvang ferociously tore it apart, spraying it with fire at the same time and disintegrating the exposed circuitry. Dree launched a fireball at another drone, causing it to dodge out of the way, and they soon caught up to Ciaran, flying wing to wing.

"Are you okay?" Dree shouted, eyeing the wound on her arm.

Ciaran nodded. "Good enough."

They split off as a Destroyer rushed between them, firing with both guns, and Lourdvang dove sharply before turning back to assist Ciaran. The pursuing drones had all stuck to her, perhaps sensing her vulnerability, and were still firing. One flew past her, and she swung her sword wildly, trying to connect with its wing; but she missed, overextending herself. The Tracker behind her opened fire, and the bullets tore directly into her back, piercing the fire-resistant armor like it was warm cheese. The force of the impact knocked her from the dragon, and her limp body fell toward the ground. She was already dead.

Dree screamed and saw Ciaran's dragon, Morningstar, roar in absolute despair before turning and throwing herself at the chasing drones. She destroyed two of them in fury before they killed her too.

"Lourdvang, we have to get to the palace—"

She saw too late that Erdath and Abelard had already

had the same thought. They were racing headlong toward the exposed control room at the back of the palace, a trail of smoke following them as Erdath challenged the drones. Abelard had his sword over his head, and he too was screaming a war cry.

"After them!" Dree shouted. "Hurry!"

Lourdvang leapt into action, following the rapid descent of Erdath. For a moment, it looked like they were following an ancient legend come back to life: Rider and dragon charging toward their enemies in the morning light, Abelard's sword held high overhead and catching the sun's rays like burning fire.

But the drones were not easily beaten.

The reserve force over the control room turned to them in unison and opened fire. Missiles and bullets erupted toward Erdath and Abelard in a great wave, and Erdath dodged frantically, avoiding the barrage. But he could not avoid them all. The bullets tore into his wings, shredding them, and a missile collided with his chest, throwing Abelard off his back. Lourdvang cried out as Erdath rolled, his eyes meeting Lourdvang's and then blinking out. Abelard fell alone, and bullets tore through his body.

"Catch my father!" Dree shrieked. She knew Erdath was already dead.

Lourdvang tore himself from Erdath's vacant gaze and went after Abe. Erdath fell toward the control room, and she saw Francis back up as he realized the massive dragon was going to land right on top of him. For a second, she thought

Erdath might end it. But one of the Destroyers careened into the dead body, knocking it aside and sending both crashing into another part of the castle.

Lourdvang continued to roar as they swept under Abe, allowing Dree to pull him in. Lourdvang launched a wave of fire toward the control room and then climbed, trying to avoid the deadly barrage of bullets. Dree turned to her father and gasped. He had bullet holes covering his side and chest.

"Dad!"

He met her eyes, and she saw that they were already clouded. "My darling Driele."

She pressed her hands to one of his wounds. "We need to get you bandaged up—"

"No," he said, as Lourdvang swept away from the palace and toward the outlying city streets.

Abelard kept one hand on his sword and used the other to stroke her cheek.

"I am so proud of you, Dree," he whispered. "You will win this war, I know it. You are more a Dragon Rider than anyone I have ever known. A Fury. My own daughter. I am so very proud."

Dree felt tears soaking her cheeks. "*We* will win this," she said. "You'll be okay."

Lourdvang landed, and he knelt down so that Dree could ease her father off his back. She slid to the ground, cradling him, and looked around wildly for help. But Abelard took her arm.

"Dree, no one can help. I'm dying . . . but I am dying as a Rider, as the man I was. And I can think of no better way to go. You gave me hope. You brought me back here. And now I go to meet my ancestors proudly."

"Dad—"

"It's okay, Dree. Oron waits for me on the other side. A Rider can ask for nothing else." He coughed and grimaced at the racking pain, and Dree saw his eyes clouding. "Tell your brothers and sisters I love them. Tell your mom . . . tell her I will see her again. Be good, Dree. I love you more than you could ever know."

Abelard's eyes widened, a brilliant blue, and then life passed from him. His body fell limp in her arms, his head rolling to the side, and Dree felt something inside of her break.

Her vision blurred and her skin erupted into fire, covering her completely. She screamed and shrieked and was racked by painful sobs. She laid her father down and climbed back onto Lourdvang's back.

"Go!" she screamed.

Lourdvang felt her rage and anguish and leapt into the air, charging into the thick of the drones. Dree's sword blazed with fire as she lashed out everywhere, and Lourdvang tore at wings and hulls and whatever he could grab. Dree stabbed her sword through a Tracker, still screaming as she did it, and Lourdvang destroyed another. They were like living fire.

But they had attracted the attention of the other drones

now, and through her haze, Dree suddenly saw the danger as at least ten of the remaining drones swept down behind them.

"Dive!" she said.

Lourdvang immediately broke toward the ground, crossing the city toward the palace. The drones closed in pursuit, firing wildly, and Lourdvang howled as another bullet tore through his wing. They had just flown over the palace walls when a missile sped past and exploded into the courtyard, creating a massive fireball. Dree saw soldiers flying in all directions, and Lourdvang was blown sideways as well, just barely keeping himself from hitting the ground. Dree wasn't so lucky. Her left hand slipped from his scales, and she felt herself falling. The courtyard rushed toward her—hard cobblestone—and she just managed to turn herself in midair to land on her feet. It wasn't enough. She hit the ground hard and felt her left leg crack under the impact. Agony swept through her as she rolled across the courtyard. As she slowed to a stop, she spotted a winged shadow as Lourdvang swept back over the wall, still pursued by drones. And then she saw the surviving soldiers closing in on her, their spears ready for the kill.

She closed her eyes, defeated. It was up to Marcus to win the battle now.

She thought she would be scared, but instead, she saw her father waiting for her, holding Gavri under one arm, and she knew she would see them soon.

Chapter 25

Marcus saw Dree hit the ground hard and felt his stomach drop. Soldiers were closing in on her fast, and they didn't look like they were going to take any prisoners.

"Nolong—"

"I see her!"

The Sage swooped down over the palace, dodging one of the great ivory towers, and then swept in for a hard landing in the courtyard, spraying fire at the encroaching soldiers and sending them all scattering for cover. Marcus leapt off Nolong's back and ran to Dree, kneeling down beside her.

"Are you okay?"

She opened her eyes and blinked, as if surprised to see him there. "Marcus?"

"Last time I checked. Come on, we need to get you out of here." He grabbed her hand to pull her up and she cried out. "What is it?" he asked, looking at her in concern.

"My leg," she said weakly. "It's bad."

Marcus slipped her arm over his shoulder and slowly lifted her. "Keep your weight on me."

"Lourdvang—"

"Still fighting," Marcus said, pointing up to where Lourdvang was trying to get back to Dree.

"We're losing, Marcus," she managed, as he helped to push her onto Nolong. "It's over."

"Not while we're still alive," Marcus said sharply, though he didn't have much hope either. He had seen Erdath go down, and then Abelard's fiery end. More than half of the Resistance had been wiped out as well, and he had seen far too much death and destruction already today. But they couldn't give up now.

There wouldn't be another chance.

Marcus managed to get Dree onto Nolong's back, and then he hopped up beside her, wrapping his arms around her. She was crying softly, and he held her close, sharing the pain with her.

"We're going after Francis," he said. "We just need to take him out. Nolong, let's . . ."

He stopped as a flicker of motion caught his eye. Marcus looked up and slumped.

There, hovering just overhead, were a Destroyer and two Trackers. All three had their missiles locked on to Nolong, and from their positions, they couldn't miss.

It was over.

"Dree, I'm sorry," Marcus whispered.

Marcus prepared for the end, and for a second, it seemed like it happened. There was a flash of crimson that blotted out the sun, and he heard the sounds of tearing metal and crackling fire. In an instant, the three drones lay scattered across the courtyard, and a massive red dragon was heading back to the sky.

"The Flames," Dree said in wonder.

Nolong jumped into the air, and they saw that a huge pack of crimson dragons were approaching from the mountains—there had to be almost a hundred of them. One dropped down beside Marcus and Dree, its great wings flapping through the air. It was Vicar, the cruel dragon who always sat beside Helvath. She eyed them, baring her huge teeth as if in a distorted grin.

"You're helping us?" Marcus asked, amazed.

"Helvath forbade it," she said. "But we could allow this no longer. We will not wait for the drones to call on us and our kin." She growled, turning back to the battle. "Besides, they killed Vero—one of our own. We had to avenge her."

With that, Vicar leapt back into the air, latching herself on to the back of a Destroyer in a fit of rage. Suddenly, Lourdvang appeared beside them, and Marcus helped Dree onto his back. She grimaced and cried out, but made it, gripping Lourdvang's scales for balance.

"We need to help," she said. "Let's go."

Lourdvang took off back into the air, and Marcus turned to Nolong.

"Get me to the control room."

Nolong flew over the palace, staying close to the white towers for cover. As Marcus had guessed, Francis had sent in his reserve of drones to help defend against the Flames. He was now left without any defense.

"Drop me off," Marcus said, grabbing his sword. "It's time to end this."

Nolong swept down a few feet from the ground, and Marcus hopped off, landing in a crouch.

Then he slowly stood up again, facing Francis from across the control room.

"You sure you don't want me to take him out?" Nolong growled.

"No," Marcus said. "He's mine."

Nolong growled, but flew off again to rejoin the battle, leaving the two of them alone.

"You have a lot to answer for," Marcus said.

Francis smiled, his hands still clasped behind his back. "Is that so? What for? Progress?"

"You killed innocent people. Humans and dragons. And for what?"

"For a better world," Francis said, as the fire and bullets swirled overhead. "A new Dracone. What more can anyone ask for? I took the office on those promises. I am only doing exactly what I said."

Marcus gripped his sword with both hands, feeling his skin heating up. "You cannot build a future on the blood of innocent people. It doesn't work that way. You are a monster, and nothing more."

"Is that so? And how about your father, Marcus? This is all his doing, you must know that."

Marcus met his eyes. "He tried to fix this. He tried to make amends."

"Did he? Maybe so. But he brought the drones here, boy. He turned them on the dragons, he created the factory and told me how to change this world: how to use steel and iron to build greater buildings and machines, how to mine the countryside for minerals and oil, and how to equip my growing armies. He told me that a new Dracone could only be built when the dragons were gone. It was his dream that I shared, and I learned from him. And you have his blood. You share in this too."

Marcus lowered his sword, shame burning on his cheeks. "I am not my father."

"You look like him," Francis said, still wearing his arrogant smile. "But maybe you aren't him. He was weak. Pathetic. He would never have challenged me in battle like this. So perhaps you are different. But it doesn't matter, Marcus. Don't you see? I know the Flames have come, but my drones are invincible. And you will die, and Dree will die, and your Resistance will die with it, just like Abelard Reiter."

Marcus gripped his sword and stepped forward. "I think you're the one who is in trouble."

"Looks can be deceiving," Francis said.

Suddenly, he turned and scooped something off the table behind him, fitting it over his shoulder in one fluid motion. It was the launcher that Rochin had used to kill Vero. "One of your father's parting gifts. That fool Rochin failed with it, of course, but what can you do? At least I get to enjoy the oh-so-delicious irony that your father's most recent invention will be the very thing that kills his son." Francis smiled. "It's almost like a song, but far more amusing than any I have ever heard, I think. Goodbye, Marcus."

Then he pulled the trigger.

Chapter 26

Marcus dove to the right as a massive fireball exploded from the nozzle, bursting into the brick wall behind him and erupting into flames. The concrete floor hit him like a truck, and he felt something shift in his still-sore right shoulder as he scrambled forward on all fours, trying desperately to hold on to his sword.

Francis laughed. "Good . . . it wouldn't have been as much fun if you died on the first shot." He stared at Marcus as he climbed back to his feet, clutching the sword in two hands. "You know, I considered replacing your father with you for a while. I suspect you could have built something grand."

"I never would have joined you," Marcus spat.

"Oh, not willingly. But it's all about leverage. If, say . . . I held Driele Reiter captive, on promise of death if you did not agree to join me . . . I think that might have worked, no? What do you think?"

Marcus felt rage stirring inside of him again. "You aren't going to touch her."

"Well, I decided I'd rather just kill her. And you. Too annoying . . . both of you. Activate!"

Two Surveyors floated up behind him from the shadows, each armed with a single light machine gun. Above them, the fight was still raging on, and Marcus heard screams and battle cries and the sound of tearing metal. He knew every second wasted was another that Dree could be killed. He couldn't allow that. If she died, then it was all for nothing. He saw no future in Dracone without her.

"Kill him," Francis said calmly.

The two drones opened fire, and Marcus again sprinted out of the way, taking refuge behind a computer station. The bullets chewed into the machinery, shooting sparks across the dungeon and shattering the screens. Marcus gasped as one bullet clipped his left arm, tearing out a chunk of skin above his elbow. Blood seeped out of the wound, and he narrowed his eyes. He needed to fight back, and fast.

Crouching low, he waited for the first drone to make the turn around the console, and then he slashed downward with all of his strength, bringing the sword right through the front of the Surveyor and smashing it into the floor. The second drone was close behind, however, and opened fire immediately, causing Marcus to again dive out of the way. He threw his sword at the drone, forcing it to dodge; and then he launched himself right on top of it, grabbing hold of the Surveyor in desperation.

The drone shook back and forth and started to zoom around the control room, carrying Marcus with it. He felt his legs slip off the ground as the drone carried him upward, and he heard the cruel laughter of Francis. The drone continue to climb, and Marcus realized it was going to try to drop him to his death. He quickly reached over, ripped off the control panel, plunged his hands into the circuitry, and yanked.

The drone shorted out, and they dropped together to the floor. Marcus managed to throw himself into a roll, taking away some of the impact, but he again smashed his shoulder into the concrete.

Groaning, he looked up to see Francis walking toward him, pointing the launcher at his chest.

"A valiant effort," Francis said. "But a vain one. Your mother was a Dragon Rider, as you know. She always liked to seem so noble . . . so brave. But she was as arrogant as the rest of them. And in the end, for all her pretended heroism and honor, it was the dragons that killed her. Fire. And so ends her son."

Marcus looked up, images of his mother and father flashing before him like a newsreel. He saw his mother standing over him, her long golden hair hanging almost to her waist, and her eyes bright. She didn't seem afraid, and he wondered why that was. Her only son was about to die, but she was not weeping.

Instead, she smiled.

And then Marcus realized what Francis had said. Fire. And a Fury would not be killed by fire.

Francis pulled the trigger just as Marcus raised his hands, focusing on the fire that had burned inside of him since he was a child. He let it wash out of him, controlled and powerful, and as the shot leapt from Francis's nozzle, it met Marcus's own energy, and the fireball abruptly stopped in midair, spinning. Francis's eyes widened as the fireball hung in the air between them, still hovering there like a star.

"How?" Francis breathed, lowering his weapon.

"I am a Dragon Rider," Marcus said, climbing to his feet. "And a Fury. I cannot be killed by fire, Prime Minister. I *am* fire."

The fireball erupted, sending Francis flying across the room. He slammed into the wall of surveillance screens and collapsed to the ground, rolling onto his back as he frantically slapped out the flames that had sprouted all over his clothes. Marcus picked up the launcher, slowly closing in on him.

Francis finally put out the flames and turned to see Marcus stalking toward him. He blanched.

"Easy now, Marcus," he said, backing up. "We can come to an agreement, I'm sure."

"I'm done talking," Marcus said, aiming the launcher at Francis's chest.

A million things raced through his mind: his emaciated father strapped to the chair for years, the outskirts of the city—ruined and decimated, the innocent people killed or forced from their homes. He thought of the people who had died in the school attack and the Resistance fighters who had been killed in the battle this morning. He thought of Erdath and Abelard, who had both sacrificed their lives to defeat Francis and the drones. And as Francis backed up, Marcus caught the glint of his dragon-tooth necklace—from one of the hundreds or even thousands of dragons he had killed. He deserved to die.

Marcus narrowed his eyes and tightened his finger on the trigger. Francis cried out, but Marcus wasn't listening. All the anger and pain and suffering had taken over now. It was time to finish the war.

"Stop!" a familiar voice cried out, cutting through his single-minded focus.

He paused, his finger hovering on the trigger. Marcus turned and saw Lourdvang swoop in for a landing, Dree on his back. Her face was singed, and her broken leg hung uselessly at Lourdvang's side, but she was alive. She looked at Francis in disgust, and then gestured upward.

"It's over, Marcus. We won."

He followed her gaze and saw that the battle had indeed stopped. The air was full of dragons, and the drones had been cleared from the sky. The surviving Resistance fighters were now circling the city.

"The soldiers are all surrounded. The drones are destroyed. Leave him."

Marcus looked at her, the launcher still aimed at Francis's chest. "He deserves to die," Marcus whispered.

Dree nodded. "That may be true, but you're not a killer, Marcus. We can't be. We have to be better than him. If we're going to build a better Dracone, we can't start like this. We can't find peace with blood."

"Now is when you decide what kind of a Rider you are going to be," Lourdvang added.

Marcus met eyes with Francis, letting his anger subside and fade away.

Then he slowly lowered the weapon.

"You're right," Marcus said. "Let's get you to a cell, Prime Minister."

Chapter 27

Dree stretched out gratefully on the soft feather mattress, still keeping pressure off her broken leg. It was set now, and the doctor said it should heal normally, though it would take time. She could walk with the splint and a crutch, but she had been ordered to rest as much as possible. That was fine by Dree. She hadn't slept well in weeks.

She and the rest of the Resistance fighters had taken up in the palace while everything was sorted out. There were homes to rebuild, people to feed, and a lot of justice to be handed out. All of Francis's personal cabinet had been locked up, as had much of the Protectorate. Even Rochin was sitting in a prison cell, facing charges of murder for Vero.

He had begged Dree for mercy, but she left her brother's fate to the tribunal.

Francis had already been charged with everything from treason to murder to abuse of office, and his trial would be held in public—overseen by the Dragon Riders, who had once again assumed the defense of Dracone. Any citizens who had taken advantage of the death and destruction of the poorer outskirts were also being stripped of their new-found wealth, and much of it was being spent to rebuild the docks and other ruined areas, including the outlying villages. She knew her father would be very proud to see the ancient order restored, though that had been little consolation for losing him. Her mother had hardly stopped weeping since she heard the news. Dree kept dreaming of his last words, and she woke crying more often than not. She and Lourdvang had gone to retrieve his body after the battle and laid him in state until the funeral.

But a small part of her knew that her father had found his peace before the end.

Dree's old school, which had been completely destroyed by the drones, was one of the first rebuilding projects, and Dree had even received the honor of naming it. The choice had been easy: the Abelard Reiter Academy. Her father's picture would hang forever in the front hall.

There was a light knock at the door, and she turned to see Marcus walk into the bedroom, smiling. He was dressed like a true Draconian now—a beige woolen tunic and coarse brown pants, as well as a sword slung at his waist.

Nolong had requested that Marcus become his Rider, and Marcus agreed happily. The two were already sailing over the city every day, keeping peace over the rebuilding process.

Marcus sat down on the bed beside her, looking over her injured leg. "How's it feeling?"

"Broken," Dree said. "But mending. How are things out there?"

"Moving along," he said, shrugging. "Nathaniel was out earlier policing the reconstruction at the docks, and we have gotten just about all of the displaced families out of Forost and into temporary homes."

"Good. It's amazing to see the city taking shape again. It almost feels like a dream."

Marcus smiled. "I know. I was thinking about where I would live, actually. Do you know—"

"Excuse me," a timid voice rang out. "Sorry to interrupt."

They turned to see one of the Resistance fighters standing nervously by the door.

"What is it?" Dree asked.

"I just wanted to ask what you two thought about the plans for the reconstruction of the docks. The teams were wondering if you had any changes. Oh, and Porter wanted to know if he can start going through the palace records to see if there are more Dragon Rider descendants in the city. Is that okay? And what about the Flames? Should we send an emissary to Helvath or . . ."

Marcus laughed and shook his head. "That's a lot of questions at once, and Dree is trying to rest. I'll come meet with you later tonight and we can map everything out. Sound good?"

"Perfect. Thank you, sir."

The man hurried off, and Dree looked at Marcus, raising her eyebrows. "Sir?"

He flushed. "They've all been calling me that. They keep asking me questions."

"I know the feeling," Dree said. She reached out and took Marcus's hand, letting the comforting heat pass between them for a moment. "We did it, Marcus. For a while I thought we were all dead."

"Me too," Marcus said. "Are you going to be okay for tomorrow?"

The ceremony for Erdath and Abelard was going to be held in the city center the next day—a full funeral procession and a resting place of honor outside the city. Dree felt her stomach tighten, but nodded.

"I think so," she said. "I know my father would be proud of me. I just wish he could be here for all of this."

"I'm sure he is," Marcus said.

"Marcus, Dree?"

They turned to see Nathaniel standing at the doorway. He still wore his black armor, and his blond hair had been slicked back, giving him a severe look. But as of late, he had barely stopped smiling.

"We have a few new citizens who are being held on suspicion of collusion. Do you think we should hold them for a few days until you're ready to see them or do you want me to question them or . . ."

Dree sighed. "Let them go for now. We can bring them in tomorrow to question them. Maybe assign Tami to handle that. She has a knack for it. But we won't be holding *anybody* without proof."

Nathaniel nodded. "Fair enough. I'll see to it personally. Feel better, Dree."

He disappeared down the hallway, and Dree looked at Marcus and smiled. "I think we might have to give up on private conversations for a while," she said. "Let's get dinner later, though. I could use a break from this bed. Where's Lourdvang? Or should I say Chief of the Nightwings?"

Lourdvang had been elected by his kin to take Erdath's place, and though Dree had to miss the ceremony, Marcus and Nolong made sure to be there.

Dree felt herself glowing with pride at the thought of her little brother leading the Nightwings.

"I saw him earlier," Marcus said. "He is still getting things organized in Forost. He asked me to tell his big sister to get back on her feet soon so she could help him out. There's no time for laziness."

"Sounds like him," Dree said, smiling. She glanced past Marcus. "We have another visitor."

Jack walked in, looking distracted. He was dressed in his clothes from home, his glasses still perched atop his nose. He smiled at Dree. "Hello, Dree. I trust you're feeling better?"

"Yes, thank you," Dree replied.

"Marcus," Jack said, "can I speak to you alone for a second?"

"Sure," Marcus said.

He squeezed Dree's hand and quickly followed Jack out of the room. Dree watched him go, and then lay back, wondering if Marcus still might consider leaving Dracone now that the war was over. She hoped he would stay, but she knew it was a decision he'd have to make for himself.

Marcus looked out from the top of the palace tower, scanning the sprawling city below. It was midday, and the sky was spotted with clouds, doing little to block the warm sun. Below was a scene of organized chaos. Buildings and stores and homes were being rebuilt, while food stands were again open for business, with new ones replacing the dragon market that had been torn down. Marcus and Nolong had been part of that process, and they enjoyed it greatly. To the east, a long line of citizens filed back into the city.

Marcus looked up and saw dragons soaring overhead, bearing some of the first ten Dragon Riders—the only ones who had survived the battle with the drones. They flew with heavy hearts for the fallen: Ciaran, Eria, Abelard, and others. He even saw a Sage working near the docks, helping move supplies to rebuild the homes. Citizens worked hand in hand with the golden dragon, and together they forged ahead.

"It's a great thing you did here," Jack said.

"You too," Marcus replied.

Jack smiled. "I feel as if at least some of my guilt has . . . I don't know, faded away. It's a beautiful world, this Dracone. And a big one. Who knows what lies out over those horizons?"

"For now, we're busy enough with this section."

"No doubt," Jack said. He turned to Marcus, suddenly serious again. "I need to head back to Earth, Marcus. I've decided to leave today. I'll track down George and make sure he's safe."

"Yeah, he's waited long enough. I'll go grab my bag—"

"You're not coming," Jack said, sad but resolute.

"Of course I am. I promised my dad I would come back for him."

Jack laid a hand on Marcus's shoulder, meeting his eyes. "It could take weeks to secure his release from the holding cell, Marcus. Maybe months. We're talking about the CIA here . . . it's going to take a lot of paperwork and legalities. You have other things . . . more important things . . . to do."

"But—"

"Look around you, Marcus. You are needed here."

Marcus frowned. Was he supposed to just abandon his father, the man he'd spent his entire life trying to track down? But Marcus had to admit—he wasn't overly keen on leaving Dracone. Not now. He was a Dragon Rider, and a leader of the Resistance. He couldn't just abandon his people either, could he?

Marcus looked away, unsure of what to do. His heart was torn: blood or duty?

Jack gestured below them, where the massive rebuilding of Dracone was taking place.

"Look, Marcus. There is an entire world to be rebuilt here . . . to become better than before. I can handle getting your father. Your place is here. I think you know that this is where you belong. I think you've known that for quite some time."

Finally, Marcus nodded. "Stay safe over there, Uncle Jack," he said, a shake in his voice. "Don't get yourself in any more trouble. I'll see you when you come back."

"I won't be returning, Marcus," Jack said quietly.

"What do you mean—"

Jack held up a hand. "To visit, maybe. But not to live. I promise you, I will save your father and I'll send him back to you. But I'm staying on Earth. It's where I belong."

"But you could live here too, you know," Marcus pleaded.

Jack laughed and looked out over the city. "I don't have Draconian blood, Marcus. I'm an engineer from Earth. It's *my* home. But I know we will see each other again, when the right storm pops up."

Marcus wanted to argue, but he knew Jack wouldn't be swayed.

"I'm going to miss you," Marcus said quietly.

"I'm going to miss you too." Jack turned and gave Marcus a fierce hug. "I'm so proud of you, my boy."

They wandered back downstairs to the great hall and saw that Dree was up again, helping her mother fix up the palace. Abi and the boys were trailing along beside them, dusting and sweeping and picking up chunks of wood and shattered brick. The palace had suffered massive damage during the battle, and Dree's mother had made it her personal mission to get it back to a "workable condition," as she called it. Marcus knew it was her way of dealing with Abelard's death, and it seemed that the whole family had taken up the cause. Marcus watched Dree straightening a picture, leaning on her crutch.

"I think you'll have some good company here, anyway," Jack said, watching the family work. "I'm happy you've found your home."

Dree and Marcus stood on the edge of the meadow, flanked by Lourdvang. Jack stood in front of Marcus, and behind him, a huge thunderstorm was just beginning to rage. Lightning raced across the sky.

"I guess this is goodbye," Jack said, his tone somber.

Dree gave him a hug, and then he turned to Marcus, who handed him a note.

"What's this?" Jack asked.

"Just something for my dad. I want to tell him that I'm waiting for him at home. Our real home. I want to make sure he knows he's welcome and that I hope we get back some of that time that we missed."

Jack smiled. "He'll appreciate that. I'll get him out, don't worry. Good luck."

"You too."

Jack turned and hurried off into the storm, the long grass billowing about his waist. The first rain began to fall, and Dree laughed as a great sheet crashed into them, soaking them to the bone. Lourdvang growled behind them, flames licking out of his mouth and sending steam shooting up.

"I'm sick of these storms," Lourdvang muttered.

"Hopefully there's just one more coming," Marcus said, watching Jack grow smaller.

"Your father will be here soon," Dree said. "I know it."

Marcus heard the pain in her voice, and he turned to her. "I'm so sorry about your father, Dree."

Dree smiled. "So am I. But I'm proud of the man he was when he died. He was whole again, a true Rider."

"I have already heard there are songs being sung in the taverns of Abelard's last battle," Lourdvang said softly. "And Erdath's final charge. They say they ride again in the night lands. I like to think that."

"Me too," Dree said softly, envisioning the two of them sailing on a cool morning breeze.

Ahead, they saw Jack jump into the lightning storm and vanish. Immediately, the storm started to clear. Sunlight soon poured in through the cracks, falling over the meadow and pushing the darkness away as if it had never been there at all. In time, there was only daylight.

The three of them stared at the tall grass for a while, letting the sun dry their sopping clothes and scales. Marcus breathed in the fresh air, letting it fill his body. It smelled of cold rain and new life.

Finally, Marcus turned to Dree. "So, what now?"

Dree smiled. "The storm has passed, Dragon Rider. It's time to enjoy our new home."

Acknowledgments

I would like to thank Marissa Grossman, Ben Schrank, and the rest of the very talented team at Razorbill for their help and encouragement throughout this genre-bending project. It has been a privilege to explore Dracone with such a supportive group. Thanks as well to the wonderful designers, copyeditors, and other unsung heroes who make sure I don't look like an idiot, despite my best efforts.

Thanks to the world's best agent, Brianne Johnson, who thankfully only started becoming recognized as such after she had already signed me on as her client. Ha! Too late now.

As always, I must thank my wife, Juliana, who doesn't understand half of what I am telling her when I am writing, but nods along and pretends anyway. (It's always nice to stay grounded.) Thanks as well to the rest of my family and friends for their ongoing and much appreciated encouragement and support. I know I say it often, but you guys just keep on showing up. That goes for the Kings, Scotts, Goodwins, Muellers, Kahns, and Niedzielas, just to name a few.

Thanks to Dave and Telma at Blueforce Logistics for always being so understanding and accommodating when I disappear into writing fogs or go on tour for my books. You guys rock.

Lastly, a very special thank-you to my parents (they also got their first dedication, which was long overdue). I write about a lot of characters with absentee parents, but mine couldn't be further from that. They are endlessly supportive, have not once questioned my career choices (which were not always logical or even possible), and are my two biggest cheerleaders by far. What's more, they have always taught my brothers and me that humility, kindness, and empathy are the most important things we can strive for, be it for humans or animals. I try to live by that and never forget that I was once a reclusive little kid reading adventure books in the corner of my room and dreaming about magic. I write every book with that kid in mind, and with the knowledge that, like then, my parents are right behind me.